DEPARTURE STORY

DEPARTURE STORY

a novel

ROWANA
ABBENSETTS-DOBSON

Edited by Alexandria Marble
Editing
Cover Design by Valentina Alvarez

Spoken Black Girl

*We delight in the beauty of the butterfly,
but rarely admit the changes it has gone through
to achieve that beauty.*
\- Maya Angelou

Dedication & Acknowledgements

⟨◆ ◆ ◆⟩

This book is for anyone feeling lonely and hopeless in the shadow of a great destiny. This book is for anyone who is in the process of knowing themselves. Most of all, this book was written for girls who don't fit in the box society has assigned them; Black girls, foreign girls, girls who don't feel "girly", girls with weird interests, girls who speak up and refuse to be told how to live this one life we've been given. Your journey is yours and yours alone. Be loud, be bright, be fantastic! Dream deeply. Feel emphatically. Scream, cry, and be human, even when it makes other people uncomfortable. Your freedom will set other people free. Anyone who has a problem with it can kick rocks.

I thank God for giving me the strength, faith, and resources to bring this book to life. Thanks to my parents who taught me to work hard and never stop believing in my dreams. Thank you to my mother, Evelyn, who taught me to be my own advocate and follow my heart, comforting me after every rejection, and celebrating every win in her own quiet way. Thank you to my dad, Rowan, who opened my eyes to the world of art and literature at a young age and encourages me every step of the way. Thanks to my sister, Deanna, who is my cheerleader, sounding board, and therapist depending on the day. Thanks to my husband Daniel, and my baby girl Symone. To both of you, I say, your love sustains me. There's no one else I'd rather be quarantined with. Thank you to the Dobson family; particularly Luberta Francis Hansley Dobson and Christina Dobson, who have made me feel loved, supported, and at home.

Thanks to everyone who has ever supported me, told me they liked my writing, followed me on social media, read a post or left a comment. Thank you. I borrowed your confidence when I couldn't feel it for myself. Thank you to the Spoken Black Girl team members who are so generous with their time and talents. Gratitude to the Black women writers who came before me and those who walk alongside me. Your fellowship, advice, and support have meant so much to me. I have to thank my ancestors, especially the women who never had the luxury of sitting down to write and publish a book about the pain and struggle they endured. They were waiting on me. Although this is only my first novel, I promise to keep writing. The past is never forgotten, it lives on in our imaginations.

I

Across the world, millions of girls are sweeping, scrubbing, or cutting up vegetables and herbs at their mother's elbow. Distracted, barely missing their fingertips, nearly knocking over a vase with a broomstick, eyes wide and mouths ajar, constantly dreaming of America. They picture America like a sitcom with lots of predetermined funny moments or like a sugary sweet pop song that plays over and over again during an endless summer. Now that I'm here, I can see that I was one of these naive girls, longing to slam a red locker door in the face of her dreamboat boyfriend just before the lunch bell rings.

But before I left home, I felt this itching to be close to my family in a way I'd never experienced before. It felt like the final goodbye, even though I knew that wasn't true. True that some part of me would go to a distant land, to learn and grow away from everything I'd ever known. But also part of me would always be distinctly different. Parts of me would be damaged far away from my mother's watchful eye, while other parts would freshly blossom. My sister, Anika, and I would always be at odds, but despite the eye rolls and snide remarks, the daily fights and the annoyance of sharing a bed with someone who sleeps spread eagle, we had our soft moments; our small moments of joy, peace, and comfort. Anika had grown even more cold and distant leading up to my departure.

I remember the day it sunk in that I was actually leaving. We were waiting for our Aunt Zoe to go shopping at Bourda Market for my trip. We sat, as we always did, in the shade beneath Aunt Zoe's mango tree, the only spot in the yard shielded from the scorching Guyana sun. Anika was painting her toenails a gloppy bubblegum pink. I noticed a ripe mango dangling out of sight just above her head. Something about her jaded beauty, her 20-inch weave cascading in waves, her long eyelashes, and button nose made me truly wish the lush, red-green fruit would fall down and knock some sense into her.

"So," Anika drawled, "You're going to America. America. You. Imagine! I guess they're just letting any loser in these days." Anika sighed, dabbing another swipe of pink on her toe.

"It's not so hard to imagine! And I'll have you know many people think I'm very cool! I can go to America!" I whined.

"Maybe, if you could have just pulled a couple of those encyclopedias you're always reading out of your tight ass... things might have been different."

"My butt is growing in, I'll have you know.... slowly."

Anika couldn't help but laugh, "Yes, very slowly."

"And I'm not sure what you mean by 'things might have been different.' ? This is good! This is what I've always wanted."

"There you go again, lost in your daydreams, Celestine. It's not real. And you're gonna end up right back here. Wait and see."

Anika shook her head knowingly, fanning the flames of my anxiety and snuffing out my fledgling fantasies all in one gesture. So much was communicated between us, from silence to a sudden noise of wounds yet unhealed. She broke away first with a disgusted blink, kissing her teeth.

"There's no way I would go to America for school. The schools there are terrible, the whole world knows that. The only good reason to go is to become a star. A singer or an actress or something like that, in Hollywood with Rihanna and Kim Kardashian."

"Really, do you think you can just move there and become a star?"

"Do you think you can just move there and become... what exactly is it you are trying to become?"

With all of my energy, I wished that damn mango would fall.

We were interrupted by the quick clip of our aunts' sandals becoming audible as she slid open the screen door and peered out, her stare alternating from Anika's heavenly angel face to my acne-ridden mug. Aunt Zoe came out onto the grass, stretching her arms upwards towards the oppressive Guyana sun as if she hadn't been born under its rays and lived every day with it wrapped around her like a blanket. Aunt Zoe had a generous smiling mouth, long hair that she always kept in braids and large almond-shaped eyes that were always smiling. She worked at the library in Georgetown and her husband, Uncle Marvin, was a political representative from the People's Party. We hardly ever saw him, a relief to me, as

I was always unnerved around him. Guyanese politics was a dirty business, and to rise to the position he currently held – it necessarily made him a hard man. Every now and then, you could see the sparks of the man Aunt Zoe fell in love with; lively, sharp, and charismatic. But mostly in his older years, fear had made Uncle Marvin small.

"Girls, ready to go shopping?" Aunt Zoe sashayed towards the girls. "Celestine, did you make a list of everything you'll need for school?"

I nodded and to Anika, as if for confirmation, but her eyes were hard again. She stood up, balancing herself on the heels of her feet on the walk towards the house to avoid ruining her pedicure.

"Shit, my nail!" she whispered a little too loudly.

Aunt Zoe's head turned slowly, as if unsure if someone had called her name and asked Anika, "What was that?"

Anika, in a much younger voice, squealed, "Oh, nothing Auntie Z!" and anything that Aunt Zoe had been concerned about mere moments ago flew out of her mind and through her ears. Walking towards the car, Aunt Zoe gave my shoulder a little squeeze. She was the only member of my family that I felt was actually happy for me.

"This is a big deal, Celestine. I remember when I left for London, what a flood of emotions!"

"Was your mother sad when you left?" I asked hesitantly. I was almost as surprised as Aunt Zoe to hear myself say it. My grandmother on my mother's side had died before I was born and I was always curious about her.

"She..." Aunt Zoe faltered, "I don't remember, I suppose so." Aunt Zoe watched me as we got closer to her red Volvo.

"Your mother will miss you very much, Celestine. It's impossible to have a child and not miss them when they are away from you. She doesn't always know how to show it, but she will miss you."

That was one of the many moments leading up to my departure that I could not help but see playing before my eyes like a silent film; even now on campus, half a world away. When my attention slipped in class, the scenes began to paint themselves like a projection over the professor, the desks, classmates. Sounds and words superfluous to the vivid memory because I have already felt their sting, my mind was already made up, the memories only brought on hurt. Some masochistic energy in my being felt a twinge of pleasure in pain. It felt like I deserved it. Like the spoonful of cod liver oil mom used to chase us down with - revolting but good for you. Bad memories were like medicine to me, drugs I would take for the rest of my life. It kept me up at night that I could not think of what I did wrong. I'd definitely done something wrong.

Although my mother spoke to me less and less as the day of my departure approached, she was determined *not* to let this chance to show off to our family and friends slip past. She decided I would have a going away party. Aunt Zoe volunteered to host and pay the expenses.

The night before, when mummy thought I was sleeping, she had kissed my forehead for so long, I thought she might have forgotten where she was and what she was doing. I could almost feel the urgency and sheer volume of the thoughts in her head parallel to mine. My throat felt tight and I feared a tear might slip from my closed lids.

It must have been hard for her to raise and try to love a daughter that was so alien to her. I was not alone in my feeling that I had been planted in this family, a faerie baby switched in the night. Where she and Anika were two peas in a pod. Anika readily embraced all our mother's interests, prejudices, and philosophies. It didn't hurt that the two looked alike - poreless brown skin beauties with baby-like, wide eyes, and easy flirts with effortless charm.

My mother only mentioned our father to say that I looked like him, dark and serious. Then she would laugh wistfully to herself as if there were some punchline she couldn't reveal. There was nothing inherently bad about either word, I reasoned objectively, and yet it hurt like a curse.

My mother radiates despair. She has no control over it, I know, and so I forgive her again and again. She gives her love like feeding babies from bleeding, cracked breasts. A weak trickle of love intermingled with the grief and loss she'd seen in her life. Her playful moments were not her loving us. When she was loving us, it was yelling matches.

When Anika dropped out of high school to pursue music, mummy gave her one good box in the ear. As usual, my brother, Joey, and I shrank back into our seats. I could see Joey's eyes shifting nervously as he thought of an excuse to leave the table.

"Uh... gotta do my homework, Ma." he stammered as he stood, turning back only to grab his bowl of soup. My mother barely noticed, waving him off with a flick of her wrist.

"Don't be stupid, girl. You're throwing away your life!" our Mother exclaimed, slapping her palm on the shaky wooden dinner table. Everyone's bowl of fish soup quivered. Her silk, red headscarf sifted to the side, exposing dark unruly curls pulled into long cornrow braids. Mummy's deep orange-brown skin was shining with sweat, her eyes like darts, precisely focused on Anika. I could feel my sister's discomfort.

"I don't care about books and maths and all that." Anika said into her soup, "It's just not for me, mom."

"Not for you? You are 16 years old, you don't know nothin' yet, little girl."

"Yeah well, I know this! I know I love singing more than anything else. And school is just a waste of time when I could be..."

"Could be what? Prostituting yourself in front of men for a few dollars? Looks fade quick enough. You'll see."

"Just because you failed, doesn't mean I will."

That was when mummy finally reached over the table and hit her. I froze. A steaming, piece of fish hung limply on my fork.

After a series of confused facial expressions, Anika started crying. One tear crept out carefully painting a luminous line down her cheek. Her eyes were blank like her body was there but her spirit had left and gone somewhere else. She stood up and left the table. *This* was how our mother loved, with the drawing of tears from her loved ones. Tears were her lifeblood.

So I was not surprised to feel her warm tears run through the fine kinks of my hair and into the cradles of my ears as she kissed me in the night.

On our trip to Bourda Market, Aunt Zoe found a dress for me. It was the kind of dress that I'd only ever seen in Anika's magazines on pale, long-legged celebrities—bright pink, draping lazily over one shoulder then hanging elegantly to the knee. We rode the wave of people moving every which way around the massive marketplace. Stalls for meats, produce fruits, spices, rum and wine, clothing and souvenirs, seemed to lean up against each other like dominoes. People laughing, cursing, and haggling for better prices. Men playing cards in small groups, smoking, and saying rude things. There was the coconut man and the sugar cane girl. Stronger than the smell of spices and sweetbreads was the smell of sweat and the breath of the people. Every footstep a reminder to the senses, a billion alarms reminding me I was alive.

The dressmaker had the misfortune of being clustered behind a meat stand, but Aunt Zoe noticed the bright cloth hanging beyond the fresh cuts. The shopkeeper was all alone at her stall. All of her dresses hung as far to the left as possible, presumably to avoid blood splatters from next door. We tiptoed over little pools of rancid blood and water. The air was stifling and raw.

Anika's eyes grew wide when she saw the skirts and dresses and her mouth might have hung open if it weren't for the stench. Aunt Zoe pointed to the magenta, Grecian dress and looked back at me smiling in the rank air as only she could.

"What do you think, Cele? This would be perfect for the party."

I stared, dumb. Until that moment, I was not the kind of girl who wore bright pink. I was never the type to play at being a Grecian goddess with my shoulders exposed. The dressmaker was an Indian girl, only a little older than Anika, with soft round shoulders and full, plump cheeks. She wore a tired old T-shirt and faded jeans, just like me.

Noticing my moment of hesitation she offered, "This dress will look nice on you, miss!"

The woman smiled and winked at me, a true salesperson. Turning to Aunt Zoe, she continued, "And she slim too, you know. Perfect! One time I have a gyal come here and try it on, but she bamsey too big, nah!" We all laughed, and before I could say yes or no, the shop owner was pulling the dress down from the display, and Aunt Zoe pulled some cash from her purse.

On the day of the party, Anika arranged my braids into a high bun atop my head. The fixture was so heavy that I could hardly keep my face at the precise angle that Anika demanded to apply make-up. She kept pushing my head this way and that way.

"Ow!" I complained, feeling an unpleasant twinge in my neck. I was afraid when she pulled out a compact of broken blue eye shadow and started swabbing it on generously with a discolored brush.

"Are you sure about this eyeshadow, Anika? I don't really wear um..."

"Colors? Yeah, I know. You just want to blend into the walls most of the time. Not tonight." Anika said, with a firm note of determination. "Close!" she commanded, jabbing the brush at my face again.

To my surprise, the touch of the brush was soft and gentle on my eyelids.

"I hope you grow out of that shyness. It doesn't do you any good." I could feel her warm, sweet breath on my nose.

"I'm nervous about what it will be like there. What if I don't make any friends?"

"You always find a group of weirdos. Now you'll find your American weirdos. You'll be okay."

I nodded my head, wanting to believe my sister.

"Watch it! Or you'll have blue eyeshadow up your nose!"

I opened my eyes and forced myself to stare at my reflection in the mirror. It took me a minute to recognize myself. The eyeshadow and red rose-colored lipstick did not look the way it used to on my features, like a little girl playing with mommy's things. I had full lips to accentuate and eyes that seemed to suggest some provocative mystery. I had a face and a body too that was forgetting about girlhood. I had my first conscious thought of being a woman. No more oversized school uniforms, cut-off jean shorts, and faded t-shirts. Just one baby bird, hoping not to starve or be eaten upon leaving the nest. I focused on the deep ochre of my irises in the mirror. I still did not know if I trusted that girl looking back, if she could really pull it off. I decided to bet on myself. I couldn't believe in anyone else.

"You'll be almost decent." I could hear Anika grinning, though my eyes were closed shut.

"Gee, thanks." I snarled.

Lively calypso music was playing from the backyard, and the sounds of people greeting laughing floated up through the open bedroom window.

I was seventeen. The age that mummy had Anika. I always told myself that when I was seventeen, I would choose better. I would choose myself and my education. I wouldn't be so foolish as to wander off the beaten path of the ones who made it out. The ones who got straight As and acceptance letters to London universities and ivy leagues in America. The ones who became doctors or married doctors. The ones who managed not to make a misstep and get dragged back down to our little paradise/hell.

I wanted to cry. I gulped furiously, not wanting Anika to see me get emotional. In our family, people were chided for crying. It made you weak. So instead, I stood up, adjusted my dress, and using my sister's shoulder I stabilized my shaking legs. Although I was unaccustomed to high heels, I was determined to have some poise. I strode to the far side of the room, gaining in confidence with every step. Then I looked back at Anika and smiled the kind of genuine smile we rarely shared. The kind that feels like your heart is exposed.

Her perfectly drawn eyebrows scrunched together in confusion and surprise. Then she smiled back, the same kind of smile, a gummy one with lots of teeth. We didn't say anything.

I walked down the stairs to see relatives arriving through the front door, women who had become aunties during one of my mother's relationships or another, their hands hot with trays and bowls of food, and old uncles who would eventually settle in a corner to drink rum and reminisce about Guyana past in between the slamming of dominoes and the clinking of glasses. Little cousins were running about, threatening the many fine bowls, crystal geodes, and vases Aunt Zoe kept on display around the spacious living room, and as I walked towards the back door, I saw that my friends were there.

At one table, the Bashirs' chatted with our Uncle Marvin, who looked uncomfortable in his leather sandals and leaf print shorts. Mr. Bashir was leaning over the table, and I hoped they were not talking politics. An Indian man and a Black man talking politics is bound to end badly so I decided to keep an eye on them. But when I passed by their table, I heard the name "Obama" ring with glee over nearly empty glasses of ice and watery rum, and I felt a sense of relief. For the first time in my memory, our upcoming national election was not the hottest topic of discussion. Instead, all eyes were on the American election. Some upstart named Barack Obama, a Black man, was running for president and by the looks of it his chances were good. It was easy to briefly ignore the tension between the People's Progressive Party, Mr. Bashirs' party, and the People's National Congress, of which Uncle Marvin was the Vice-Chair.

I caught sight of the young people. Cousins and friends were knotted together, balancing plates of pine tarts and delicate-looking cheese straws on their knees. Joey was hitting on my friend Marissa. She never told me this outright, but I knew that he was the reason she didn't want to come over anymore. Marissa stood up immediately, came over, and hugged me.

Before she could sit down, other cousins and schoolmates were coming up to hug me. All commenting on how beautiful I was until I felt I'd rather die than hear another surprised compliment. I don't think it was the make-up or the dress that drew them to me. The scent of America already hanging over me was like a pheromone dripping from my pores, spilling out hope, luxury, and ease. Although I could not be sure of any of those things, I sometimes indulged in the fantasy with others. The whole party was running on fantasy. Because if not this, what did one mean when they said they hoped for better things? I turned back to Marissa complaining about my brother.

"He is *disgusting!*" she fumed. "Telling me about how we gon have a baby and ting." She made a wrenching sound.

"He's joking, Marissa." I said in a soothing tone, all the while shooting my brother a dirty look from across the party. He smiled and shrugged nonchalantly.

Kelvin stepped into the party quietly. He had a gift for going unnoticed that was painfully familiar to me. Perhaps that was why we would never be the way he wanted us to be. I wanted to be excited about a man. I wanted to get to know the intimate secrets of someone different from me, who lived a different life or at least knew there were different lives to live.

Kelvin had been my schoolmate since primary school. He was my first school dance date. He was the first boy I let kiss me. His mouth tasted like sticky sweet coconut water after we shared one near the sea wall. Our first date.

He was nice enough, but so readily available. From years of watching my mother try to build happiness like a house of cards and watching it fall every time, I got the sense that life was never so easy. But I entertained him at times. I even let him touch my non-existent butt a little bit.

One night, only a few weeks before my going away party, Marissa and I went to another going away for a popular girl in our year with wealthy parents. She was going to study in London. Her announcement effectively stole my thunder, but I didn't mind. At her party, Kelvin, Marissa and I had one hell of a tropical punch. The rum ran nearly pure at the bottom of the pitcher. He touched my butt again, but this time reached his hand between the cheeks, stroking me from the front and back again. I still remember how I shuddered. And maybe this was the reason why I'd given Kelvin a chance the summer before I left for America. But as soon as we started this thing - sloppy and not totally pleasurable kissing with teeth and drool, him timidly touching my body in places I'd never been touched before, me waking up to text messages filled with x's and hearts–I began to feel repulsed by his presence. And as the pressure began to build to go "all the way", I found myself itching to leave the country as soon as possible. I would rather be remembered as a great love who was lost than the girl from across the street who broke his heart.

Kelvin was wearing an impeccably ironed plaid shirt and his regular day-to-day jeans, faded at the knee. He was growing into his brother's clothes now, I thought to myself. He would not like to hear me say that out loud. The truth was that the boy with eyes like a scared doe was growing handsome, his jaw more pronounced, his skin was clearing up. I had even heard a rumor that a girl was jealous of me. Over *him*. She should have taken him. They both might be happier that way.

"Hey, baby," he said, pulling me in by the waist after a moment of awkward hesitation. I hated it when he called me "baby". I was *not* his baby. That is not to say that I wouldn't have been someone else's "baby", but certainly not *his*.

"Hi Kelvin," I said, forcing his hands off my waist and taking a step back. I was embarrassed to have this display of affection in front of my mother, although she had so much wine that she barely seemed to notice. I didn't want mummy to know a thing about a kiss, a touch, *or* a boyfriend. That was all Anika's territory.

Aunt Zoe rushed towards the center of the lawn where a little clearing was still free.

She yelled, "Hello, excuse me?" into the buzzing crowd and then a sharp "Quiet!" which made everyone jump because she did not often raise her voice. Soon only the light clinking of glasses could be heard against the soca tune that the DJ turned down low.

"I was just thinking let me make a little speech, you know? This girl here, but eh, she's a woman now right? This woman Celestine, she is one of the brightest minds I have ever met in my life, and I can't tell you how happy I am to have her as a niece."

She stopped for a moment to dab away a tear and I felt my own eyes prickling with emotion. To my Aunt Zoe, I owed my survival. She was a place to go when I wanted to be with someone or if I wanted to be alone – she always knew which one I came for. But best of all, she made books accessible and unlimited to me. It was only a matter of asking. She let me study in the library after hours although she wouldn't let me get any studying done. She liked to hang around my table, ask me everything about my life. And truthfully, I liked telling her. No one else really cared.

"When I tell you this is a special girl – she has so much ah life in her! From small, she always like to read and write. Hours pass and ya nah hear nothing from she! Because she have her head in the books!" Aunt Zoe laughed, throwing her head back.

I liked it when she talked like this, forgetting her "librarian" voice. She was not usually so boisterous, but I guessed that the liquor had been flowing for some time before I came down to the party. Everyone already seemed sated and merry.

"Like you." My mother's voice floated in from the far end of the yard where food in tin pans steamed. Candice and Zoe had a complicated relationship, I could never quite figure it out.

My mother loved her sister, and yet resented her for her seemingly charmed life. She loved her sister and yet hated her for loving me, the child she had purposefully neglected. But her voice was not harsh, yet it seemed to take everyone in the party a second to realize that Candice was not chastising her sister.

"Yes," Aunt Zoe picked up. "Like me. In some ways, but in other ways, Celestine is all her own. This child since young had wisdom. Since young she ask me "Aunty why this? Why that?" Or she know when to hush up and listen. Ya hear me? Since young she wise." Aunt Zoe's eyes began to well up again, and she called me forward, placing her hand on my shoulder. I looked out at the party assembled in the yard. Joey leaning up against the mango tree, already bored, Anika indiscreetly texting, old aunties I rarely saw watching me more intently than I had ever been watched before. Next, my mother took the mic, not to be outdone by her sister.

"I always knew she was meant for something different than I know about, so I ... sometimes I did not know what to say."

The party was quiet. It seemed the whole of Buxton just then turned off to be quiet.

"I do my best for her, my best might not be good enough, but it's what I give. And I hope

I taught you strength for this journey ahead of you. I didn't mean to – I only wanted you to be strong. This place heh we livin, I've seen girls like you smart and beautiful, snatched from her dreams just like so." Candice snapped her fingers and the sound echoed through the yard.

The effect was chilling, but mummy was still smiling.

"I wanted to protect you. I see now you can protect yourself. I know you'll be successful, Celestine."

2

Just the way I had nervously made my way down the stairs to my going away party, I made a similar voyage the night I met Richard. I descended the staircase, shrugging past wallflowers glued to their phones and radiating anxious loneliness, and a drunken couple making out, the girl's skirt hiked up and the guy's hands swarming all over her. I look away, embarrassed. I pause on the landing to survey a real-life American college party. The couches in the living room have been pushed to the walls to make space for dancing and a fierce game of beer pong. The line for the beer kegs intermingled with the line for the bathroom. I could feel the energy of so many connections happening, so many judgments and lapses in judgment, generating this physical buzz that hummed above the music and the alcohol. My head was full of this buzz as I surveyed the crowded first floor of the house on the Simon College campus I shared with three other girls.

Richard Wirth sat with his knees together and feet in-turned, legs jerking up and down erratically. There was something about this posture that I chose to read as eccentric and mysterious. His glasses might have been plastic, but they didn't look cheap. I had been watching him study in the library all semester, his glasses hanging askew on his narrow face as he poured over piles of political science periodicals. We had bumped into each other a few times around campus.

Richard was the kind of white boy I could imagine myself with – eyes and mind so open and well-intentioned that one would think he was dropped as a baby by his ultra-liberal professor parents. I could tell that he'd never thought twice about college – whether he would go, whether he would get in, or whether his family could afford it. If I feathered his brown curls with talcum powder, I could easily imagine him sitting with a student in his own office, musty with the smell of books opened once a year to keep abreast of things.

I used to think that I could lose myself in that kind of academic, white liberalism. That I could maybe forget. And that the white liberals would be forgiving of me, you know, for being dark-skinned and foreign. They might even relish it.

So, I decided I would be his wife. I would live with him in a modest, comfortable home not too far into the bramble of off-campus. And although no one would say so, my brown skin next to him would make him more eccentric and strange. I was willing to do that, though, to become an unspoken exhibit, if I could have a taste of the carefree life that Richard did not even know he had.

But who would I be? Besides a wife? Back in Guyana, I always thought I would be a primary school teacher –a good, safe career. I would keep up my strict regimen of reading the newspaper in the mornings, then a history book at night and hope to remain satisfied that way.

But ever since I had arrived in America, constant anxiety seemed to strum on my spine day and night. Something had changed. Now, a haze had fallen over my vision for my future.

Now, I was marrying Richard – or rather marrying his access to books and lectures. The prospect was enthralling.

"Richard, Richard, Richard!" Gerty teased, pulling the two of us aside to an empty corner of the kitchen, "You remember Celestine, don't you?"

"Yes, I think so. From World History every Monday, Tuesday, and Thursday since January."

"Aren't you observant!" she exclaimed, grinning from ear to ear. Gerty danced around us, tipsy, always ready to engage, her hair still wet from the shower.

I smiled shyly, now wishing I was as drunk as Gerty. In the morning, she wouldn't even remember this interaction. Someone in the growing crowd called her name and she started moving towards the living room. She gave me a tiny wink and mouthed "HAVE FUN" as she disappeared into the crowd.

Richard held his hand up as if for a shake, but then quickly withdrew it, wiping his palm on his jeans.

"Sorry, my hands are sweaty."

"It's hot outside, so that's understandable."

Our eyes were locked. He looked at me in a way I wasn't sure I'd ever been looked at before; as if I had value; as if I was a prize.

I wanted to speak, but I was frozen, rooted to the spot. This happened sometimes, my voice abandoned me, leaving me with this tight feeling in my chest, my airways were suddenly the width of a bendy straw, and my belly would writhe around as if trying to escape and find a new body. I couldn't recall if I had ever experienced this feeling back home, but ever since I'd come to stay on campus, these episodes occurred at least twice a week. It took everything in me not to run back to my room and phone Aunt Zoe crying like I usually did when these feelings came over me.

I shifted my weight left and right, self-conscious in a skin-tight black dress and strappy black heels that pinched my toes. In Guyana, they might have said I was easy for wearing a dress like this - it might have cost me my safety or even my life. But here in America women were liberated and could dress however they chose without fear, or at least that was the conclusion that my favorite American television show, *Sex in the City*, had given me. I envied the self-assuredness of the women here, knowing they were protected.

But now, standing in front of Richard I felt that I had tried too hard. What I hoped would be enough for most men seemed superfluous when I saw him. His wiry frame was hidden beneath an oversized band shirt which read *"The Clash"* and jeans. His black, rectangular glasses were his only accessory. That was the thing I couldn't understand about Simon College kids, they were so insecure, but they had nothing to worry about. They thought so little of themselves, but they were America's chosen ones with opportunities plentiful as blades of grass.

I, who had known nights rumbling with hunger that rang in my bones. I, who had seen floods try to reclaim my grandfather's home two times over and seen the land reclaim his grave in one long rainy season. I could not relate.

Earlier that evening before the party, Gerty rattled off what she knew about Richard Wirth.

"He's an international studies major," Gerty said, nodding

knowingly. I was international, so naturally, he would be interested in studying me as well.

"He lives in Matterson, you know, near the Deltas, but he has a single room." she tittered and winked.

I could not really distinguish between most of the campus frats. They were sunburnt white boys in tank tops and baseball caps – who belonged to what Greek symbol, I did not know and did not care. But Gerty knew. She could read off the members like her Spanish conjugations – haltingly, but completely.

She knew the most about the Deltas because this semester she had fallen in love with their president, Jason Steinhart. Richard was an acquaintance of Jason's and lived in the very same hall. These two things gave Richard value in Gerty's eyes. She made it her business to encourage our flirtation.

"He also does, like, film or photography. Wait, no – he's in the Film Society. Is there such a thing as Film Society?"

"I have no idea." I lied. I happened to know that he was the club treasurer, but Gerty probably wouldn't find this as charming as I did. She struggled to open a bottle of seven-dollar chardonnay.

"I'm taking a buzzed shower," Gerty announced.

"That sounds dangerous," I said dryly, picking at my glitter nail polish. It took a minute for me to think anything of Gerty's silence. When I looked up, she was glowering at me.

"Try to have fun tonight," she urged, "You've been so... stuck lately." She sounded uncomfortable. Gerty did not like to talk about the fact that we didn't really like each other anymore.

"Stuck, am I?" I snorted with laughter, but spotting

Gerty's tightlipped pout, I said, "Maybe you're right. Finals are coming. It must be the stress." I smiled sweetly.

Gertrude Allen had a plan. First, a buzzed shower (chardonnay bottle precariously placed atop a toilet seat) which would lead to a fun time getting ready with their other housemates Caitlyn and Margo, carrying her smoothly into a crazy pre-game, and then, of course, the party itself would be a swimming success. Gerty had purchased three handles of vodka to ensure this.

"Shots tonight!" she said like a threat, grabbing the wine bottle and striding off towards the bathroom.

Instead of a buzzed shower, I opted for a nap. I climbed up my usual two flights of stairs, and slightly haggard, fell onto my narrow bed. Sleep was my one escape. I did not have to think when I was asleep and thinking seemed to be all I could do during my waking hours. Not just about schoolwork, but about how to be and what people saw while I was figuring out this process of being and whether or not they were really seeing me at all. Being awake meant continuous striving for... something I was not sure what.

It was too hot for May. The air conditioning had not yet been turned on and I woke up hazily from one of those stifling summer sleeps. My cell phone had made its way between my shoulder blade and the mattress amidst tossing and turning. It was vibrating angrily.

The screen said *"Home"*. Home. How rude of that place to show its face here. Without the heart to end the call before it even began, I let it ring.

Why wouldn't they stop? I didn't want to tell them directly that home was not home anymore. I just wanted them to get the hint, but they kept forcing it. They kept saying "need" – that they "needed" me at home. Apparently, halfway across the world in a flood-damaged house in Guyana, my presence was absolutely required.

Since last June, when I said goodbye to that place "Home", their calls had become more and more frequent and the topics of conversation had changed. They used to be "How is everything is America?" and detailed questions about American life and American celebrities that my mother seemed convinced I would bump into with time.

I remember one of my mother's first calls since I had left Guyana and come to a little, old brownstone in Brooklyn. I stayed with my aunty Sylvia, my father's sister, in Flatbush for a few weeks before my orientation began. Out on my auntie's fire escape, I let my toes dangle through the bars and laughed with my mother like I'd never laughed with her before.

"Try an see Obama, gyal." She urged me over the crackling phone line. Her voice felt so good in my ear.

"But mummy, Obama doesn't live here! It's DC you talkin bout."

"But he does come there sometimes! To New York! Isn't that so?"

I laughed. Ever since I got my acceptance letter, her affection for me began to blossom. Eighteen years too late, her love had ripened with time, smelling of regret and shame. But it felt good to be loved like one of my siblings – like Anika the singing beauty, or Joey the charmer. My imminent departure from the land that we loved despite itself somehow created value in me. Perhaps I would be Celestine the ascending, carving my way out of the lush land with a cutlass, victorious over poverty, victorious over shame. Or maybe I was just still Celestine the reader, Celestine the dork. Or simply Celestine the provider, with the promise of American prosperity on the horizon.

Anika sent me a Facebook message saying mummy's latest man had up and gone over to the neighbor's house to add insult. Now that another one of my mother's boyfriends had taken off, the calls were rolling in. The conversation was less sunny now. My mother, sister, and brother liked to call me and then talk about what another one of the group really, desperately, needed and why I should provide it for them. It used to be money.

"I hear you making big money over in America, Celestine."

My brother Joey called during orientation. Right in the middle of ESL tutoring that I did not need. I still remember how peculiar it was to hear the shit-grinning smile he had to have been wearing over the line. It would not have surprised me to find that Joey thought everyone was handed a burlap sack of money upon first stepping on U.S. soil. Somehow, it had escaped my family that although I was going to school in the U.S., I was still broke. Even with my sizable scholarship, I still had to work at the Provost's office for a few hours a week, which made me just enough to buy overpriced fraps at Starbucks in the mornings and order pizza on Saturday nights. I made these purchases my new "normal" frivolous ways to prove to my classmates that I was, indeed, one of them. I may speak with a foreign accent, my skin is dark, I don't eat bagels and I'd only ever seen squirrels in a zoo until last year, but I can make a Starbucks order as if it is my native tongue. The expense of pretending leaves nothing to give away. I tried to explain this to my family, but they refused to understand.

Placing the vibrating phone on the windowsill, I pulled back the thin twin XL sheets and felt some relief from a warm breeze wafting through the window.

I dreamt of Richard – a man I felt I could take seriously. A glowing force behind my closed eyes. He was always reading some frail, old book or staring all consumed, into the screen of his new, chic Mac laptop. I dreamt of him typing furiously, and his shapely arms tensing with concentration. In the dream, I was the only one who could break his concentration. He looked up from his computer, his eyes met mine and then he would look away, flustered, but smiling with his lips tight.

The dream was modeled after real life. We had been flitting eyes at each other around campus and finally, this spring semester, he happened to be in the same World History seminar as myself and Gerty. We were both history majors.

He ran in circles close to ours, or at least his friends did. Richard had been close with Alex Turner in the first semester. Apparently, they grew up together and applied together from the same high school. But when Alex began hanging out more with Gerty's beloved Jason Steinhart, the two friends grew apart. Richard had a group to which he could belong if he wanted to, but often chose to be alone.

His friends made regular appearances at house parties around campus. Richard did not. One could not simply bump into him in a socially sanctioned act of drunken lust at 3 p.m. in the library. Gerty made it a point to include him in our study groups to give us time together. Or more likely, she hoped to attract Jason to our table in the library with

Richard's presence. She never studied and continuously texted me about how he was looking at me and trying to flirt, and why didn't I flirt back?

There was something about learning Tudor era foreign policy and the panicky feeling of almost certainly falling in love that felt exhilarating and dangerous – like drowning in the Thames and coming to life again at his elbow under the library's harsh, white light.

I felt this thrill now in bed. It made me reach for my thighs, then between my legs rubbing upwards with a firm, flat palm the way I wanted Richard to. My door banged open and I quickly put my hands on top of the sheets. It didn't really matter. The room was dark, and the only light came in above my head by the window. And anyway, it was my friend and housemate Margo. She was drunk and more focused on making her way across the room without falling over than thinking about what I was doing.

"What time is it?" I pretended to be groggy, but really, I'm not sure that I was ever asleep, just daydreaming with my eyes closed.

"It's, like, 9:00," Margo said. Americans peppered in the word "like" so frequently, I wondered if it was a secret code word. I quickly learned that it was a filler for silence, a stopper for awkward moments where one might be vulnerable or say something real.

"Ella is here, so Caitlyn is fuming. And Jason's acting like he doesn't even see Gerty." She laughed a gurgly laugh. "I would too, she looks like a fucking mess! And this is coming from me!"

Margo's head lolled to the side with drunkenness and she

took another swig from her mason jar. Her lipstick was already smearing, but other than that, she was her usual wild, dark-haired beautiful self. Margo sat down on the floor next to the bed. She was wearing a red mini skirt and a flowy, lace top –her going out clothes.

Of the housemates, Margo was the one that I liked the best. She was kind-hearted, open, and understanding. She would talk to me about anything that crossed her mind, from live updates on the status of her parent's divorce to the movements and behaviors of her secret pet iguana that she hid every time the college maintenance workers came by. Her family was from Venezuela, but Margo was born in the United States. Fellow students would ask her "Where are you from?", perhaps detecting something foreign in the shape of her eyes or the way her peachy skin turned bronze in the sunlight. She would say, "Lake Station, Illinois" and laugh as their faces changed.

Margo had a perfectly well-adjusted group of friends in the drama department. She stopped by their table sometimes at meals. They were not as flashy as our group. They did not hang with the unremarkable children of C list actors or wear the latest preppy fashions. Margo seemed happier with them but felt indebted to Gerty for lifting her out of obscurity freshman year. We both felt the same kind of Stockholm syndrome. Gerty rolled her eyes whenever Margo went to hang out with the theater kids.

"What are they doing anyway?" She would sneer, "Running lines?" They probably did and I couldn't think of what was wrong with that.

Margo nudged me with a blue-tinted mason jar filled with

pinkish-orange liquid. I pulled up the sheets. I was only in my underwear, but most of the American girls didn't care about that sort of thing. "We're all girls!" My housemates would squeal as they applied makeup and I squatted over a questionable toilet seat at some frat house.

"Relax, Cell. It's just me!" Margo giggled, already drunk. She offered up the drink once again, some of it had sloshed onto her hand but she hadn't noticed. Before I could ask she slurred "It's punch!" She winked.

Margo placed the wet, sticky jar in my hands and watched me expectantly. I knocked back the punch – a too-sweet orange drink, grapefruit juice, and the better half of one of the bottles of vodka had gone into its making.

"God!" I grimaced. Margo smiled triumphantly as if giving drunkenness was to give a gift.

"Now, get ready! Do you want to dance with Richard with that bed head?"

It was true that my hair was sticking up in the back. I touched it subconsciously, my roots felt thick and coiled in my fingers. I rolled my eyes laughing and shooed Margo away.

"Hurry up!" she moaned, "He looks like such a loser just sitting there alone."

"Don't call him a loser!"

"He is!" she teased, "Hot loser, though." We exchanged mischievous smiles, and she sauntered out of the room.

I turned on the light and stumbled to the full-length mirror that hung on the back of my closet door. It was always a shock to see myself. I spent so long avoiding mirrors that I could barely recognize my own reflection. Dark brown skin like my father's, or so I was told, too big eyes like my Aunty

Zoe and a narrow nose that my mother bragged came from Portuguese ancestry. I ran my fingers again through my braids, gathering some resolve to face the world again.

Richard wanted to dance. He led me to the small living room area where the furniture had been pushed to the walls and everyone was grinding to a Lil Wayne song. People here thought that I should be able to dance, but back home when I danced at all I liked to wine, not grind. I'm sure that grinding had come from wining, but there was no art to this American dance, no *sensuality* or rhythm. Wining is like the meeting of mutual indecent thoughts, dancing that makes you want things your mind refuses to articulate. Most of the boys here could not even be bothered to get on the dance floor. They stood against the wall while girls gyrated on them and they sipped beer from a solo cup. Nothing could be further from dancing to me. Where was the drama? Where was the element of over-the-top, boisterous, corporeal expression that made dancing seem like a fever that brought on instinctual, sensual behavior? American parties, in general, were so far from the fun that 90s movies had promised that I was already getting over the party scene. But unfortunately, I lived with Gerty, who seemed ready to drink and party as frequently as she possibly could. It was coming to the point where we were all sick of it and

Gerty had to pressure us into having drinks with her. But on this night, I was grateful.

I did not expect Richard to dance the way he did. There was nothing at all wrong with it, it just wasn't the way boys usually dance. First of all, he did not pull me in close to his body. We danced face to face and he had moves. His movements were elastic, one side of his body was always reacting to the other half a second later. The word that came to mind was "fluidity". It was contagious. I started moving loose and fast too. The whole time he looked me in the eye with such intensity that I was sure he was trying to read my thoughts. The music changed to dubstep and electronic. I could tell he was in his element. I couldn't help but admire his stamina.

He danced until dark circles formed by his armpits and his face glistened beyond his black frames. He looked really free, like his brain had happily slipped out of his left ear. I wanted him to touch me, but I knew he wouldn't just yet.

I pulled him over to a makeshift bar that had been set up on the kitchen counter littered with used and unused solo cups scattered across the kitchen island, slops of orangey punch spilled over from a giant bowl, somebody's lighter, a mostly empty bottle of cranberry juice, and a towering bottle of vodka. Richard regarded the dwindling cranberry juice for a fraction of a moment, and then eagerly suggested shots, prepared to endure the burn of cheap vodka rather than using the last of the Ocean Spray cranberry juice. I didn't enjoy taking shots, but observing his reasoning it seemed only right.

The cheap liquor tore down my throat with the precision of a fresh paper cut and I struggled for a moment with the urge to spit it all up. I was relieved to see the same grimace on Richard's face – his cheeks deeply pink, his mouth open in disgusted disbelief of what he had just consumed. But the first shot having gone down, we both were feeling brave. When Richard, still red in the face, suggested we do another, little fractals of light shining dangerously in his colorful corneas, I agreed –and he lifted the heavy jug of vodka to pour tiny portions into our shot glasses.

And because of the first shot, the second one wasn't so bad. I spun gleefully, felt the vodka sloshing in my stomach like gasoline, like fuel. I felt ready for whatever was to come. I felt daring, prepared as if I could go for miles and miles with not even the faintest idea of a destination. Richard had an idea of a destination.

"Let's get out of here," said Richard, still breathless from dancing.

I hesitated, unsure.

"I...Gerty needs me to be here... she's upset." We both searched the room for Gerty and found her bent over in giggles at so-called-heartbreaker Jason's side.

"We don't have to like, do anything." He said, embarrassed. I was relieved to see that he was just as confused by the rules of hook-up culture. I nodded in appreciation. "Cool."

"But it's so freaking hot in here and it smells like pure B.O. How about some fresh air? Have you ever been to Cloudy Point?"

3

I'm not insensitive. I'm not a "selfish bitch" as my sister liked to call me under her breath. I know that my family struggles sometimes – the luxuries of gas and electricity come and go with each month's fortune. The house itself was crumbling before our eyes with no money for repairs. Where the foundation met the ground, it seemed to crumble into the reddish dirt itself. The house, my house, was now a faded bright coral and had the optimistic aura of a cheerful home. Eighteen years before, my father had chosen the cheapest bucket of paint, which happened to be garish pink, violent magenta. It's hard to believe that we used to be a happy family just like any other. I was the baby, my father's favorite child, or so I've been told. I can't remember for myself.

The women on the street pointed at our house and laughed, not even bothering to hide their mocking from my mother. In a better life, this bright pink house, faded to coral by rain and unrelenting sun, would have been a magnet for fortune. Its color would have beckoned luck and good spirits. But it's so easy to thwart what could have been, what never was, and it seemed as if my family had managed to repel this slim chance.

My mother inevitably cites a fifteen-year-old back injury whenever her latest man leaves and I suggest that she should work. I know that Joey could help if he spent less on rum and weed. My sister, Anika, can sing like an angel, and could easily work a part-time job between gigs if she wanted to. Instead, they reminisce about the days when they divided my meager check amongst themselves.

In Guyana, I worked as a secretary for the local real estate agent, Mr. Bashir. When I was in the 7th grade, I saw his advertisement for an after school, part-time position on the school bulletin and called directly using the principal's phone. The idea of working had always captivated me, mostly because it presented itself as an alternative to being at home.

Before then, life had consisted of Joey grunting for food as if he were the big man of the house, with all his immature, stoner friends hanging around. I could not even sit on my own bed since Anika often kicked me out of our shared bedroom. She would slam the door shut and screech whenever I tried to enter, haphazardly throwing the book of my request into the hallway if I banged on the door for long enough.

I never felt the relief that a daughter should feel when their mother comes home. Mummy doted on Joey, who was so handsome, and so good at impersonating a gentleman that he could do no wrong in her eyes. But she knew very well about Anika, who did the bullying for her, clinging desperately as mummy was to the idea of good motherhood.

I wanted to know worlds outside of that one. I *needed* to. The need hasn't subsided since. To think that the repellence started as early as primary school when I would volunteer to help the teachers wash the blackboard after school, to now, in America, where I have finally minimized my family to a mild buzzing on my phone, was extraordinary.

At the age of fifteen, I became Mr. Bashir's assistant, creating Excel documents on Windows '98 and organizing his dilapidated file cabinets. I rarely got more than a third of my paycheck after my mother and siblings cunningly extracted their share. Mr. Bashir and his wife seemed to know this somehow and tried to do what they could for me. Mrs. Bashir would send a plate of food down most nights since they lived on the floor above the office – hot bowls of dhal and steaming pholourie with sweet mango chutney sauce.

Mr. Bashir was a very learned man and he was pompous about it. He had been a lecturer at the University of Guyana for twenty years and taught at the University of Calcutta for two. That was where he had met Mrs. Bashir. After deciding to retire from academia, he opened a small real estate firm. He liked to question me about whichever book he saw peeking out of my school bag.

"What's that you're reading?" he would ask, too casual.

He liked to reminisce if he had read the book or snatch it up hungrily if he had not, reading the blurb on the back with mistrustful eyes as if any book that he did not know about must be of a dubious origin. He liked American novels and collected old westerns. He lived for anything that showcased brazen, splendorous, American freedom. He was well-read also in Guyanese history and literature, but the fantasy of America was a fervent side hobby. He clung to tidbits of gossip about American celebrities and had rigged the little television at the back of the office to catch some American channels. Dramatic notes of *All My Children* could be heard faintly each afternoon.

It had been Mr. Bashir who, through his university contacts, had learned of the full-ride scholarship that a small liberal arts school in Indiana happened to be offering to worthy international students. He was the one who read and re-read the statement that I had to submit along with my application.

He wrote one of the two recommendation letters required – a document that somehow had stretched to six pages. I applied without really expecting to get it. My secondary school grades were impeccable, but with Guyana's underfunded education system, that could only mean so much.

I expressed my concern to Mr. Bashir about a week after I submitted the application, wanting to soften the blow before my rejection letter arrived. He had been watching *Law & Order* on the pixelated television in the back room, his tea growing cold in a saucer at his elbow. I had been getting ready to go home after a filling meal of roti and lamb curry. I stuffed the two foil-wrapped dhal puris Mrs. Bashir had forced into my hands into my rucksack as I stood in the doorway. I liked to talk to him when he did not appear to be listening. It was easier for me to speak freely on topics other than books when I thought he might not really hear. But he always did.

"I probably won't even get it, you know," I tried to sound casual. "Why would they want some nobody from nowhere?" I added a little false laugh.

He continued to watch the show with rapt interest, and I turned to walk away.

"That is why they will want you." he said absently. I paused in the doorway for only a moment to process his words. Then I stormed out, gnashing my teeth and breathing fast. He was supposed to reply that I was not nobody. It was one thing saying it to myself, but this? He was one of three people I could trust to lift me out of self-pity, but not that night. Humiliation crept into my lungs, making it hard to breathe.

The night had come suddenly and completely in the few hours that I had been at the Bashir's. Even if I had enough composure to see, it would have been difficult in this absolute darkness. My mind could only fumble for revenge. I stopped, shaking as I took my rucksack off and felt through it for the warm, foil wraps. That was it. I would throw the fresh dhal-puris down in the road for them to find in the morning. Never mind that their giveaways were usually my breakfast and lunch for the next day. I gripped around the bag, touching my books, folders, and various loose papers.

I did not hear the whirring sound of bicycle wheels or even the urgent chiming of a bell. The first thing I felt was the worn rubber braising my right leg, which crumpled instantly under the stinging pain. Then the fender tore into the exposed skin just above my knee. The bicycle toppled over. The cart that had been attached to the back and the bundles of sugarcane it contained toppled over as well. Sugar cane rolled innocently into the road. The man who had been riding got up, already angry. He looked down at me. I was not bleeding too badly, but enough to redden the faded, cracked asphalt beneath my right leg.

"Get up gyal!" He was maybe forty, his creased, dark skin shining in the moonlight, his lips pursed as if he had just tasted something foul.

"Ya hear me, gyal? What the hell you tink it is at all? Come offa de damn road!".

He pulled me up roughly by arms. I wobbled a little on my right leg.

"You okay?" he asked, still angry but with kindness fighting through. He had me lean under the awning of a variety shop, staring at me with a concern so intense that it frightened me.

Here I was, a nobody, making trouble.

A car passed behind us blasting lively dancehall music. It missed his bike narrowly but ran over the long, green stalks of sugarcane. The man looked back at the scene, one hand still supporting me. He shuddered involuntarily and I could feel his pain, potent as if it were in my own heart, by the slow way he tore his eyes away from the scene. He focused on me again, even more ardently this time.

"Where you live at, gyal? Ah – Ah – Ah could try an take you dere, you know." He must have meant well, but I was shaking.

My hand trembling, I touched the parted skin above my knee. It came away dripping. Fleetingly, I thought, loss of blood. Could that be why I felt so faint? I touched more of my exposed leg. My knee highs had long since slackened to my calves. I remembered with a feeling of tragedy and loneliness that I was a woman and hurt and young and stupid. I felt small.

The man held me firmly by the arm. I felt caught, helpless. Where was I on the spectrum of power? I was a girl who was crying in the night against a shop and had not even gained the courage to speak a word.

I heard quick slapping sounds and then her voice was upon us. Mrs. Bashir was in her rubber sandals that she kept by the stairs. She clasped both of my shoulders in her hands. The man let go of his hold on me and Mrs. Bashir stared at him. She started jerking her head towards the road as if she meant to shove him from where he stood.

"Listen, miss," He started, "I ain touch her." That was all he said as he moved towards his bicycle again. By some miracle, it had not yet been run over. He walked to the bike and cart slow, stood it upright and jumped on, pumping off in one smooth motion with no intention of looking back. He left the damaged sugar cane by the roadside.

I was convulsing in sobs. Mrs. Bashir, a slight woman, struggled to support me even though I was a twiggy, little thing. She made continual shhing noises, sounding more frightened than me even. Mr. Bashir was running up the road towards us. When we met up with each other, he tried to pick me up and carry me, but I clung to Mrs. Bashir. We tugged her between the two of us until he gave up and settled for helping his wife stay upright.

I sat on the bright yellow stool that Mrs. Bashir had placed in the corner of the kitchen. It had been so placed to allow Mrs. Bashir to write poetry in thin, papery notebooks while some smells of her home in India and other smells of here plumed from pots intermittently. It was a special place, and she plopped me down there nervously, her eyes unable to look away from my leg.

Mr. Bashir shuffled to get the few first aid things that were around the house – an unraveling ball of yellowed bandage tape and a bottle of Dettol. I had never seen Mr. Bashir like this before. He seemed to be moving so slow and yet he could not make his hands function properly. He fumbled with the bottle of Dettol and poured a little onto the kitchen floor instead of the rag that his left hand held out for it. Mrs. Bashir stared at him for a few seconds, which in my memory feels like a lifetime. She looked a little confused, a little curious, like she was working up the question to ask when he put the rag to my thigh and I screamed in searing pain.

Mrs. Bashir deftly slapped his hand away.

"You mix di ting with water?!" she screeched, overcome by his foolishness. She only spoke in Guyanese patois when she was livid. Mr. Bashir's eyes bulged like a frightened child's.

He left the room. In a minute, we could hear the click of the TV turning on again, then the jingle of a McDonald's commercial.

Mrs. Bashir nursed me with such tender care that I could not stand to feel her fingertips. She was so gentle moving a wet cloth across the excess of blood. She was so careful where she dabbed, and when she put the diluted Detol onto the wound, deep and wide and open like a shark's mouth, she only dotted the bruise gingerly. Just for an instant, I wished Mrs. Bashir was my mother. Then my tears sprung up anew.

Mummy stood watching Mrs. Bashir and I enter the living room with a look of amazement.

"Eh eh! Is what happen to ya foot, Cele?" She held a curling iron which was clamped onto a lock of hair. The rest was gathered up in a braid sticking out of the other side of her head. She had her silk, purple robe on which she only wore when she was preparing for a date. I could see that she only wore panties beneath the robe. I could not meet Mrs. Bashir's eyes. My embarrassment made the pain in my leg infinitely worse. Mrs. Bashir guided me to the couch and helped me settle into the seat.

"Goodnight, Candice." Mrs. Bashir said pleasantly.

My mother did not know what to say between my bleeding leg wrapped up like a zombie and Mrs. Bashir's first and last visit to the house in the five years of my working for her husband.

Ignoring my mother's silence, Mrs. Bashir turned to me. She held my hands in hers. Her hands felt strong and bony. I remembered the quick force of her hand from earlier. Pale on the palms and rusty brown on top. She leaned over and whispered to me.

"They will want you because you're a dangerous girl. A smart and dangerous girl." She smiled mischievously. She understood more of me than I did. Dumbfounded, I smiled too.

My mother was so transfixed by the whole scene that only a few seconds after Mrs. Bashir left she screamed, "Oh Shit!" The curling iron had burned her forehead. It would leave a mark.

"An wah ya gon an done to yourself, gyal?" She looked into a tiny vanity mirror belonging to Anika. Before I could catch my breath to respond she said, "I always tellin' you not to spend so much a time at these coolies you know!" She kissed her teeth.

A twinge of anger rose in me, nearly cracking me in two, but my voice was still gone. By then it had been a few years since I learned that "coolie" was not just another name for an Indo-Guyanese, but a racial slur. My mother said it so often, her boyfriends and their friends did too.

In the bedroom that Anika and I shared, I sat at the edge of our twin bed. Anika was singing along to Beyonce's latest album as she had been continuously for the past two weeks. The last notes of "Sweet Dreams" faded off and Anika seemed to come back to her senses. She looked over at me sitting stunned on the bed. I felt her eyes on my bandages. She at least had the decency to stop the next song from playing.

"What happen?" she asked flatly as if she were entitled to know. I tried to tell her what happened, but she kept repeating back things that I had said in question form.

"You got hit by a bicycle? You just walked out into the road? A sugar cane man helped you up?"

I remembered the man and was ashamed and embarrassed. "And then Mrs. Bashir brought you home like a baby?"

My chest tightened. She was always ready to go, and I, somehow even after seventeen years in Anika's company, never was. You couldn't tell whether her next words would be sweet or sour. Two years older than me, it seemed that I could never be more than a young brat to her.

Truthfully, we were both childish. It felt as if my quips about her being vapid and dumb did not penetrate her skin as deeply as her snarls of "ugly" and "friendless" stung me.

I stretched back on the bed, moving aside a few strong-smelling bottles of lotion and bits of a chandelier earring fallen apart. The room was made girlish by Anika's presence. The two piles of books stacked to the ceiling in the corner of the room were the only sign of me.

I knocked her lotions and potions off my side of the bed. She hurried over to pick them up, cursing me loudly all the while. My head on my pillow, I listened for the rhythm of the night, grass rustling gently with snakes and rich air vibrating with wings, all drowning out the sounds of Anika's hissy fit. Drowning out the sounds of Joey coming home and mummy complaining to him about one thing or another. My head might as well have been underwater when I listened to the night. I grew gills and breathed. It was necessary to my protection.

I fell asleep so quickly in night water. That was what I called it, where I told myself to go. To the night water. Where the slamming of the screen door could not ring in my ears, where it did not matter which strangers were in the living room or how loud they got. The unfamiliar fighting voices of men were mere mumbles to me. The sounds I could not stand, mummy crying late at night, so gently I should not have been able to hear, but I did, I drowned out in the night water. Anika crawling through our flimsy bedroom window, the swollen wood of the house creaking under her full figure. Sounds of pleasure (those I could stand the least).

That night, I thought about America, really for the first time, and I was scared. I knew loneliness, but nothing like this – moving thousands of miles away to live in a place where not even my daily annoyances could keep me company. I was going to a place where I would doubtlessly encounter unknown problems.

I knew about America. I'd read enough of their textbooks and I'd even read some of the texts they keep out of their textbooks. The only conclusion that I came to understand was that there was much to understand. Every country has much to understand, but this felt different.

I knew that my skin was dark brown, that my hair was all spring and fuzz and I knew that meant it was harder there. It meant it was harder here too. I read about the turbulent politics and tension in the Georgetown Chronicle. But I was comforted. I did not think that one could erase the other.

We had no queen to jump, no possible checkmate in this world. We were all but pawns, black and brown people fighting their own skin, the afterimages of dreams western empires once dreamt. Still dreamt. And I was going where the dream was still alive, apparently. One of the places where whiteness still roosts, tired of our hot sun and wild, knowing land. Sure, there were others there, but on TV and in the movies we got to see, it seemed there would be so many perfect white families there, living on miles and miles of stretching suburbia. Unless I was in New York, or LA. But I was going to Indiana. I was scared to be the only black girl there.

The school would be adopting me — their own foreign baby to be held up like a beacon. In the night water, I heard Mummy's new man come in. He was vexed because she's taking too long. He's vexed about everything. His name is Sammy – what a stupid name for such a big man. I said as much one day and mummy twisted my ear so tightly I slept on my other side. She was devoted, that woman. It was a shame that either she could either not stand the church or the church couldn't stand her. She could have been a deacon at First Light Anglican Church down the road where the other mothers worshiped.

"Move ya rass woman! Come see your ting is right here. Pick it up nah man!" I didn't have to know what they were talking about not to like it. It didn't matter what they were talking about, really.

It ate away at me hearing Sammy, only the latest in a series of men who had been parading in and out of our lives for the last ten years, have a go at my mother. It was eating away my capacity to love. I felt for certain that I only had a finite amount of feeling to feel.

Sometimes I felt as if I were close to being depleted. I was becoming hollow. Lately, things were hurting more as they grated on me. I felt that I was in my final weakened state. I could not hear Sammy or whoever yell abuses anymore. I could not see her hurt anymore or hear her cluck her tongue when I asked what was wrong. I was already hollow or stuffed like a doll, either way not quite important enough to feel. I was not sure how much longer it would be until I gave out. I was scared of what giving out meant.

"*If... if...*" I sang in the night water. "*If I do get this scholarship, I will have to take it. Gather yourself, Celestine.*" And in my mind's eye, I was out in the deep, black, night water, my neighbor's guinep trees were an unknown species of seaweed. The frogs in the damp grass were sea creatures surging forward. I looked down at my own body, translucent but still dark in the absolute night, and I gathered. I gather tamarinds, brown like me, and the nice soca songs that were about Mash, the bent Guyana gold ring with a "C" engraved on it that my grandfather had given me at the age of six. His history books that were brittle and gathering dust long before he died were my first obsession. The books were the reason I tried so hard to learn how to read, the reason why I borrowed the school dictionary so many times that the librarian eventually just told me to keep it. The books sat right on top of my heart, heavy and unavoidable in the night water. Next to them, the sweet jelly insides of coconuts and the smell of vegetation and dampness that clung to my skin in the rainy season.

I wanted to gather a sense of self, an armor against the

forces that I knew I would be coming up against in the future. I wanted to think that I knew something about myself before I entered a world so vast and unknown that it might take from me what I did not know I had. Despite Mrs. Bashir's encouraging words, her husband's comment still haunted me. Even into the night water. He was right, though. I knew that my acceptance letter was coming. I was even more rare and special than an African international student. I'm from Guyana – a land forgotten by my grandfather's European history books. Even if Portugal was worn proudly worn in the loose curl of my mother's hair. Even if we talked of the Queen of England as if she talked of us. The more I pieced together about the world around me, the more I came to resent the acceptance letter that would arrive six weeks later.

The idea that I was so insignificant in the eyes of this American institution that raising me to the status of college student would be the boldest feather in their cap infuriated me. But they had me. They hadn't even made the offer yet, but they had me. Their glossy brochure promised a kind of ease of life that I had never seen. A life filled with ardent learning and indulgent relaxation. I had no better option. I could not afford to be indignant. Slowly, my fury crumbled. Hard feelings fell away, and I started thinking about the potential for a new life. Far away from "Home."

At the end of my freshman year, I was alone. Alone in a state that I had never heard of two years ago, nestled in the heartland of a country I had only ever thought of in the abstract. When my phone lit up again, vibrating with renewed zest, I simply turned it off. "Home" disappeared.

4

We turned off the main campus thoroughfare onto a faint dirt path that led behind the art building. The earth was tilting, growing steeper and steeper. Richard took my hand and helped me over the old, rusted railing that was supposed to prevent students from going further, but was so low to the ground and decrepit that it could hardly be called a barrier. The grounds, however, were still wet from the rain a few days gone, and there, in the great campus beyond, gnarled roots jumped out from equally old and ugly trees that blocked the moonlight. As if I had stepped through a black veil, he became my only reference and shred of familiarity. And how thin a shred he was. I thought to myself *"Richard, he lives in Matterson, International Studies."*

I let these blank facts comfort me even as Joey's grave warnings of white people who chopped victims up and hid the parts in tree hollows rung out in my head.

"They say we the killers, but I rather get shoot up or stabbed, than die without my fucking limbs."

But my whole way of being was based upon me not being that Black girl who things happened to, so I shook away these thoughts. The face of Lucy appeared – a Kenyan girl whose name was continually dragged by most of our class due to a drunken incident in which she confessed her pain to a rather ugly, blond, frat boy. Her face was multidimensional like a hologram before me. I closed my eyes in the darkness, opened them again and she was gone. Richard and I struggled in brambles and fallen trees to a bright clearing up ahead. My hand was in his, rougher than I had expected, his grip tight like he really cared if I fell.

"I can't believe you've never been here before!" he said breathlessly. He was invigorated. By the time we made it to the bench that was perched at the edge of a plateau, we were both winded and sweaty but inexplicably laughing. Whether we laughed at ourselves or together it was hard to be sure, but the mystery of it put a charge into the air. I could see the same charge in the finality of the blue sky and in the blinding motions of stars. The interstate highway ran hundreds of feet below. The mood was nearly endangered by my realization that my foot was only inches away from a used condom, but then Richard pulled out a joint. He too could not stand to let the moment leave us.

He presented it between his pointer and middle finger. Not giving it to me, just holding it between us with a question mark looming up somewhere in the night sky. And I nodded and laughed. He started laughing again too and we heard our echoes reverberating off the trees and the asphalt of the highway running below us. Then, with a sudden air of seriousness, he lit the thing. A stoniness (no pun intended) crossed over his features. He inhaled, his brow still furrowed, then looked at me with an earnestness that was almost painful and passed it. It was not my first encounter with marijuana. My best friends at Simon College used it regularly as a kind of lame rebellion against their parents who had probably done the same thirty years before. I took a hit, my scarlet lipstick painted one end when I passed it back. It was rough going down, but the pain was better than the alternative – being inside of my own nervous, insecure self.

The taillights of the cars that passed below grew bright, then ran like colors in the wash.

"You know what this feels like?" Richard asked wistfully, his eyes not quite focused,

"Actual fucking honesty."

I was struck by his brazen "F" in "Fucking" and the impact of his statement - how quickly my mind had registered it as true. It was forceful.

"That's what I like about this place," he continued, "the people mostly suck, but even they can't mess up the pure beauty of the place. Not just the campus either," He took another hit, his voice growing tight. "Just look at the stars," he said looking up suddenly, "And the farmland... so much fucking farmland, and it's all in pitch darkness, you can't see the horizon. Just stars."

I felt it coming up in my throat the way that it had come up so many times before, although less and less frequently now – the need to talk about home. My lips parted reluctantly, "It's like that in Guyana at night too..."

There was silence then, and I thought it might be the typical awkwardness of saying you're from a place that most American eyes glaze over on a map until they think *"Do you mean Ghana?"* as if I could be misinformed on my own birth country. I looked over at him. He gave a bored, impatient nod, as if to say "AND..." and I realized that I had left my statement with such an unfinished air that he was only waiting for the rest of it.

I laughed. "You can't see your hand in front of your face at night. I think only the mosquitoes can see."

And he laughed a laugh that I instantly identified as joy directed at me rather than anything I had said. Him enjoying me.

"So, how does it feel? Being here... for you?"

My mouth had been dry before, but it was worse now. No one had ever thought to ask me this all year. I knew that my expression must be betraying my cool, but I thought that I might cry just then.

"It's been like cheating on a lover - one you thought you were really done with."

"My, oh my!" Richard smiled wryly.

"It can feel just that melodramatic sometimes."

"So, are you enjoying it? The affair?" he asked in a false whisper. He handed me the joint.

"Not really, that's the most tragic bit about it. I thought I was but, I've realized that... But then, maybe it's just me."

He shook his head "no", wistfully, almost smiling, and then I felt I didn't need to say anymore. I struggled in my clouded thoughts for a moment. His manner made us feel equal – two disillusioned college students.

But I had not felt equal to anyone for so long. I could not tease apart which of my identities was hurting – my race, my foreignness, or my sex. Maybe all of the above. But I felt it when I pressed my edges down flat when I said an odd phrase, when my accent was too accented when I talked back to the boys when I begged to disagree. The rare moments that I hated in which someone asks, "Is this how they do it in Guyana?" as if Anglo-Saxon practices and values had yet to find me in the bush. As if they could watch my family eat dinner on *National Geographic*, surely, I had hidden rituals and ways. But I had been raised to be like them. Cellphone wanting if not cellphone having, addicted to the internet and determined to have a passion. I could tell that I disappointed some people. It might not have bothered me quite as much if I had not stayed with my aunt in Brooklyn before starting at Simon.

Walking through the streets of Crown Heights, she showed me the plain racial divides as one reads a history textbook – not indifferent but helpless and removed.

I did not know what I thought America was before. I knew that Black and brown people were oppressed, but on the flip side, it seemed like there was so much opportunity – certainly more than I would have in Guyana. That reminded me of how little I had. And so, I came to America with a spirit determined to beat it. Celestine versus America. I knew that if I worked hard enough, I could have whatever I wanted. But by the end of the summer, I realized that America did not work that way. There were people, brown and Black people, that were being killed, incarcerated, invalidated daily.

On campus, I became aware of those who tried to minimize my struggle in this picket-fenced town, where it was largely thought that struggle could not take root - that the soil could not accommodate it. I prepared myself daily to snap and had been, in the privacy of my dorm room imbibing raging levels of Malcom X to the sounds of Nina Simone. In public, I carried myself with careful but threatening dignity - as if daring any soul to muss my peacock feathers as if I had been gladly waiting on it. I wanted to feel that my burden was equal to Richards, but I fought back the dull feeling in my now numb tummy, that he could never know how completely exhausting it is to be me and how I had been exhausting myself without pause since my birth in a former, little known-throw away British colony. I wanted to shed these heavy layers - foreigner, female, and Black at that, but I was finally beginning to realize that there was no shedding it. There was only the ongoing fight for legitimacy - the fight to be enough.

In Guyana, there were racial tensions, but it was more akin to two young children aspiring to be like the colonial parents. The Guyanese population is largely made up of Blacks, the descendants of African slaves taken by the Dutch, and Indo-Guyanese brought over as indentured servants from India by the British after the abolition of slavery. Years of colonial rule created a kind of Stockholm syndrome relationship with the British, never mind the fact that western powers even after colonial rule manipulated the two groups to struggle for power against each other. But outside of the realm of politics, they had learned to shared one culture, and besides the sibling-like pokes and bickering, one group never aspired to the other. Both looked wide-eyed to the phantom of the British Crown. But in America, the past and the present mingled uncomfortably. The only options seemed to be to ignore it, as so many comfortable white Americans like to do or to live in constant rage or self-doubt like so many Black Americans do. I came to this country with the ludicrous ideas that my mother had planted in my head that we (i.e. members of the former British Empire) were better than Americans, especially the American Blacks who she mostly knew through rap videos. But ironically, amidst the wide range of inequalities that America shoulders - inequality is the great equalizer for Blacks. No one cared that I was born in a different country, or that I was more partial to cricket than baseball. In one glance, it was easy to deduce that I was just Black - an equal part to one blanket "Black" race and one social status.

My face grew hot as I thought about these things. It occurred to me that there was a good chance I might start crying. Instantly, the specter of Lucy sent a chill down my left side as if she had just come to sit next to me on the wooden bench, an embodiment of my disgrace. I bet it had happened just like this with the ugly blond fratboy. They had just been talking, post-coital and still drunk, the epitome of vulnerability - and her loneliness in this friendly college town finally broke her. Inches away from companionship, it broke her.

Richard was taking a deep pull and ashing the jay as if it were not his first rodeo. His expression was grave, but then he said, "You're beautiful." and I smiled and mouthed thank you, but didn't believe him. How could I? I had been pleasantly surprised when I got to campus with how enamored everyone I met seemed to be with me. One thing people liked to tell me was "You're beautiful. Where did you say you were from again?" For a long time, I didn't mind it. I was flattered. It was rare for people to call me beautiful. I did not hear it from my mother whose only comment on my appearance tended to be that my skin was too dark and that my hair made me look like a bush baby. My auntie Zoe would tell me all the time that she thought I was beautiful, and not because she thought that I needed it but because she thought it was true. She said it so casually as if it were fact.

Richard shifted awkwardly on the bench and I thought he

would reach over and kiss me, but instead, he put his hand over mine, and this was much, much worse than a kiss. My eyes were stinging either from tears or the effort of holding them back.

In the middle of my struggle, Richard tore his eyes away from me and stared at the winding road far below. Red, blue, and white lights were flashing, illuminating our faces. A campus security car moved along the road slowly, two officers with flashlights flanked both sides of the vehicle. They were looking for something. We watched, engaged deeply as only high people could be in this situation. What were they looking for? Who? We spit-balled possibilities - a drunken runaway? A lost deer or rabid raccoon? It spoke to the culture of the campus that these two possibilities were very real to us. Simon College was synonymous with intellectualism, nature, and unabashed drunkenness.

"Might be the Cardinals," Richard offered. He was not talking about birds, but the eccentric quasi fraternity unique to Simon College - an organized band of only the most unusual white, struggling poets who enjoyed cult films, psychedelic drugs, and flannel. They often had celebrations in out-of-the-way places on campus with acoustic guitars and heavy drug use.

"Or a murderer..." I teased in an ominous voice.

He laughed. "Celestine, I would never think to accuse you of having a dark sense of humor."

"Well, why not? You've only just met me. How could you know what kind of humor I have?"

"That's true," he said. "It's just I always imagine you as sweet."

"Sweet?" I scoffed. I did seem sweet from a distance though, didn't I? "You imagine me?"

I said slowly, smiling toothily. Richard bit his plump lip and blushed to look up at me guiltily. "I do." He said quickly, apparently unperturbed.

"For how long?" I demanded. I was surprised to find myself so brave with him now that he had as good as said it.

"All year." He was beet red now, the flush spread up beneath his glasses.

"Okay," I said matter-of-factly, "I just needed to know the exact magnitude of this moment."

"I'd like to know too. But I guess you never said you imagined me. Maybe you don't."

"I wouldn't be here if I didn't. When I don't like a boy, I don't like a boy. When I do, I do." I said simply, looking down at my ravaged nails.

"Do you always talk in riddles while you get others to confess?"

Somehow that felt like a compliment to me. But as I smiled, I reflected. Maybe I only spoke in riddles because I was afraid to speak with my voice. This thought disturbed me, and I was sure it would be more entertaining to be wry and flirt.

"Mostly, yes. I think I like it better that way."

"You really think you're so inscrutable?" he said as if he knew otherwise. I was taken aback. He seemed so shy and guarded from afar, from the small talks we had together on the way to classes or when we met in the Starbucks each morning (Richard liked coffee, I liked oversweet lattes and nothing else). He always seemed tight-laced and I hadn't expected him to be so honest with me.

I was a little scared to tell you the truth. I had failed for a moment to keep some guard up, and I hadn't even known it. But why was he bothering to know any more than what I presented to him? It was frightening but pleasantly unusual.

"I... I don't think I would say that. No one's a complete hard shell, I think."

"But you can do it, though, just consistently deny other people the opportunity to get to know you."

"Someone will break through." I realized, then, that this was what I really wanted for myself, for someone to break through. He was smiling a little.

"Sounds like *you're* the one who thinks he's inscrutable."

He laughed, leaning back on the rickety old bench. His loafers, worn, faded things, were covered in mud. I hoped it meant he would finally get rid of them. Everything else in his quirky style of dress I could abide by. His oddly square and flat gray school bag, the fact that he wore vests, those things I had already put aside – I was deep in the work of loving him and neither of us really knew it.

The quiet of our world was disrupted by the sound of heavy footsteps struggling through the woods behind us. With it came the crackling noise and muffled voices of walkie-talkies and varying Midwestern accents, squeaky to deep.

"Looking for a Black female, about 5'7, 130 lbs." We heard through the dense trees.

Richard quickly outed the half-smoked joint on the worn wooden bench, then threw the thing into the front pocket of his book bag as if it were a pencil. Something about the sound of the description made my heart jump into my throat and I was frozen still as the steps approached noisily. They shone a flashlight in our direction.

"Officer?" Richard asked, surprised and polite. The three of them shone flashlights in his face, then the three spotlights moved onto mine.

The leader of the pack, a thick-shouldered man with a struggling comb-over, considered me for a moment. I knew that it had been his voice speaking. There was something about the way that these people, especially the town people that worked around campus said "Black". It heightened my senses and immediately made me cautious and calm, nervous and irrational all at the same time.

"You Celestine Samuels?" The leading officer asked. He blinked back any awkwardness he might have felt, but his ears were still glowing red beneath his security cap. Even in the night, I could see that.

"Yes, I am." I said in a measured voice, "But I am not as tall as 5'7 or as heavy as 130lbs."

Richard laughed a little too heartily.

I remembered with a drop in my stomach that we were high and drunk. Richard gave me a quick, unsure look. He wondered if he should take over. I ached for him then and loved him more for offering his unassuming white boy mug up in my defense. I loved him for knowing that it might be necessary. But I nodded at him – one short curt nod so that he understood I would take care of it.

"I am Black, however." I finished, not knowing what else

to say. The description they gave was still playing again and again in my ears.

The officers fidgeted uncomfortably. The female officer stepped forward, indignant in the face of my humor.

"Well, that's the description that your mother provided, Ms. Samuels."

"My mother?" Those were the last words that I expected to hear from her.

"Yes, she called and said that she hasn't heard from you in three weeks."

I wish the cliché chirp of crickets did not ring out through the darkened woods. I could feel Richard's surprise and confusion beside me. Campus security officers shifted their weight uncomfortably in the heather.

"Yes, I… we got in an argument," I said in a closed, choked voice. The three officers and I all exchanged looks one by one, then the leader of the group, who seemed the most stern, cracked a smile.

"Kids, man," he laughed and looks to the others, who immediately seemed more at ease.

"Reminds me of my Sarah. I try to tell her she ain't grown. She loves that silent treatment game." The others chuckled guardedly.

"Alright now," he said, cutting off the laughter he created. "You got a cellphone? Why don't you give her a call?"

I nodded and whipped out the prettiest prepaid phone at Walmart while everyone watched me. I fumbled for the bright flimsy calling cards that I could only get in Indianapolis. I brought each close to my face in the pitch-black night.

"This one is expired…" I mumbled as I examined the next

one. I kept at least two on me at all times just in case I needed to call home in an emergency. But since I had been calling my family so infrequently of late, I was having a hard time keeping track of which ones were out of minutes. They all looked so similar, the green, yellow, red, and black flag, a tropical bird here, a jaguar there. My ears were burning with embarrassment as I sorted through.

The lead officer cleared his throat. "Ahem... why, why don't you... Just make sure you give her a call, okay, Ms. Samuels? Tonight, alright?" He tried to sound kind and fatherly. "Okay," I said obediently, "I will. Thank you, officers." The officers nodded briefly.

"Goodnight. Goodnight, son." he said addressing Richard specifically, his gaze lingering.

As soon as they left, I shoved the calling cards back into the forgotten pocket of my purse. I would call her alright, but not now, not here and not in front of Richard.

I lifted my eyes to his, which were already on me, waiting.

"I'm sorry about all of that."

If my eyes had been stinging with isolation, fear, and pain before, it was nothing compared to the prickling impulse that was now making my eyes water. Water. Already running with my eyeliner and tracing a path down my cheek.

"Please don't," he started forward, raising his hands up towards my face, fingers twitching, unsure. I nodded. I knew now that I could speak to him without speaking and he would understand.

"I haven't been talking to her, to them..." I made myself keep meeting his eye – kept wishing he'd blink. But he was just nodding at me. Richard couldn't stand my cliffhanger confessions. Where most people lost interest and moved on to what they were thinking about saying while I was talking, Richard was still at attention. It was unsettling, how badly he wanted to listen to me.

"I understand. I feel the same way about my dad. You need your distance." He said lightly as if it didn't hurt. I knew it hurt for him, but secretly it felt good for me that he knew this same kind of pain. He turned to face forward again and looked out over the peak.

"You're closer to your mother?" I asked tentatively, hoping to lighten the mood.

"She... she's dead." He spat it out. I could see a spasm of pain travel across his features, making his eyes wince and his plump lips grown thin. We were both very still and quiet. A pickup truck passed on the road beneath us. I felt a feeling like my belly had been cut open. There was an invisible throbbing in my abdomen and the feeling of things falling out and the frantic feeling of stuffing it all back in again. I did not know what to say to him. Here I was not speaking to my mother and Richard's mother was dead.

"You closer to your father?" he asked. It took me a moment to hear him and when I did, I went very cold. I felt my skin grow goose pimples in the night. "My father," I began, uncertain, "He is no longer..."

I couldn't say it. "In my life." I didn't want to be fatherless. I didn't want him to see me as fatherless. But Richard nodded again, smiling a smile that threatened tears. "We're in the same boat then."

I didn't know another person's words could catch in my own throat that way. A sinking feeling washed over me. I was a coward. I should have just said it "My father is not in my life now. He *left my mother when I was six years old and I can't tell whether my memories of him are real or memories of photographs.*" I couldn't say those things, and yet I knew that he was misunderstanding me. I was a coward.

He moved his thumb in one quick, tender motion over my right cheek, wiping my tear away. *Again, I thought, this is the kind of white boy… this particular white boy.* I was numb inside, but I could feel the night again on my skin. Once Richard and I clambered out of the dark thicket and up above the rail guard, I had a run-in my stocking that spanned the length of my leg. I looked down to see how much of my leg had been exposed. Even in the darkness of the night, I worried about Richard seeing the gash on my thigh, smooth, dark and shiny now. The last thing I wanted to do was explain that I had been hit by a sugar cane toting bicycle. No one at Simon College had seen this scar. I sometimes fantasized about Richard being the first to see it, how it would feel when he touched it, but not now and not like this.

We walked along a dark, backroad towards the dormitories clustered on the southeast side of campus. It would not have been difficult, in theory, to turn to him right now and tell him that my father was alive and probably happy somewhere without me. But I just couldn't. It was our first time, uh, hanging out or whatever this was. Would that be the first thing he would glean from my personality? Dishonesty? I wanted to spend more time with him. Immeasurable amounts of time. That could not happen if I told him that I had lied, insulted his mother's memory with my falsity. I

could not think of firmer grounds for never speaking to anyone ever again.

Between that crippling guilt and the fury that licked up
my sides thinking of my mother's daring nerve to call the
school and ask for me, I was barely conscious of my surround-
ings. Every now and then I glanced nervously at Richard, hoping he would still be there despite my inattention. He too
seemed to have retreated to his own little world. The night
had given us both a lot to think about. In my flats, my feet
grew damp with grass dew from the expansive lawn. I did not
even have the sense to shiver.

Oh, I would call my dear mummy alright. I would call her
and let her know just how alive and well I was. Somehow, I
blamed her for my lie too. I blamed her for having me through
the usual means resulting in the births of children, for her being a woman and him being a man and her not – not honor-
ing my life enough to keep him in it no matter what. But hell,
I could not even be sure that I was lying to Richard. If he had
passed, I doubt it would have ever met my ears. Not even in
death would mummy manage to talk about him at any length.
I blamed her for my shame, for his utter anonymity. I blamed
her for no photographs. I blamed her for no stories and I
blamed her for making him nothing but a dark-skinned man
who made a dark-skinned daughter. It was no small thing to
call another human being dead before their time. My eyes
stinging with tears, I let him be dead.

I wanted to point a finger like Anika and I did when we
were small. At age eight, Anika's shoulders were perpetually
sunken by the prospect of the belt.

"It's she who do it, mummy. Look how she break up my

dolly, mummy!" And she pointed her finger at 5-year-old me. It never worked out so smoothly when I tried this. And now I wanted to point a finger at Candice Samuel for every time I was denied leniency and delicate treatment. I blamed her for every time the eraser slipped while disappearing my father and rubbed wisps of me away with it. Richard's hand was sudden and warm on mine.

"Celestine?" he called, concern in his voice. I blinked, looked up at him and then all around. We were at a fork in the road. His dorm was to the left and mine to the right. I wonder if he held his breath at this the way I did. But I had no patience for questions and he honestly looked so uncomfortable that I could tell he was not in the habit of having ladies up for a night cap of warm beer from under his bed. I liked that.

"Goodnight -." I started. I'm sure I must have looked crazed just then. I had been staring so intently off into nothing, consumed with a "home" that clung to me, that my eyes must have been red with strain. He did not seem put off my forlorn features, however. He was moving his hands outward slowly as if they were levitating against his will. He did not seem to know what to do with himself, only that he should do something. Make a signal or a sign. Wanting to end his embarrassment, I ran into his arms to give them something to do. I was worried he seemed so attracted to despair. He spread his hands respectfully across my lower back and kissed me. His lips were as plump as they looked, but also as chapped as they looked too. And I had only ever tasted one other mouth before his, but I was pretty sure after only one kiss that he might have had honey on his lower lip it tasted so noble and sweet. We pulled away. The clop of footsteps broke our reverie for the second time. Students' faces still hidden in the dark, approached. We exchanged looks, gave garbled goodbyes, and went our separate ways.

5

❧

Even hungover, I could not sleep well at night, and with the evening's events playing again and again in my mind, it was no surprise that my mind could not settle down to sleep.

We kissed! Yes, but I lied. But we kissed!

Nothing could surpass that fact; I was now convinced. The only thing that kept creeping up was the fact that my mother had sent campus security looking for me. How desperate. How embarrassing. How... I did a little grunt. It felt good, like when Anika and I would communicate in animal noises. That fond remembrance made me forget her worse qualities for a moment until I finally found a calling card that would work and she answered the phone.

"Hello? Who dis?"

"Anika, it's me."

"Me who?"

"Give mummy the phone. She called the school asking for me?"

Anika laughed her piercing laugh, "Yeah, that was funny eh-eh?! But why we can't find you? What happened to your phone?"

"It's..." I didn't want to say, but I didn't want to lie. "Give her the phone!" And abruptly, it was my mother's voice that I heard over the line.

"Why I can't hear nothing from you? Why?" Her voice thundered over the crackling line.

I felt a familiar sort of fear wash over me, almost comforting.

"You all are harassing me!"

"Harassing you, eh? Is I who is harassing you? I am your mother!"

I pulled the phone away from my ear and then drew it close again, afraid that Gerty would wake up in the next room from the noise. It had happened once before, I had been on the phone with home at some strange hour and Gerty had come to the door silently, listening. I happened to glance towards the door and see her there. She smiled enigmatically and I cut my argument with Joey over sending him the new Jordans short. I had been glad of the excuse. She told me that she could not sleep and wanted to take a walk. That had been a better time between us, but not now... By the time I put my phone back close to my ear, Mummy's anger was turning into something else.

"I just wanted you to know. She say don't even worry you with it but, I know you woulda want to hear."

"Wait, what? Hear about what?"

"Zoe. She in the hospital. Gunshot wound to her shoulder. I think they gon let her out soon though. Doctor said about two, three days. And uh... and Uncle Marvin is dead." I felt numb and heavy one moment and then shaking with life in the next.

"What... what happen?" My voice came out girlish, but I was too dazed to be embarrassed.

"Some government goon set ah bullshit." Mummy said bitterly. I wondered if she really knew the details or if she was just too upset to say.

We spent two whole precious phone card minutes in silence, grieving together. I longed to feel her rub the back of my head, fingering my curls as if they were her own personal crops. It was the way that she touched me when she saw that I was sad. She cradled my head as if I were a soft-skulled newborn baby. Maybe she missed this simple motion as much as I did. So on top of the shock and grief there was knowledge of how far apart we were. "Zoe's going to be fine. Just a shot in she arm is all." It did not seem so light to me.

"Still, I should see her and go to Uncle Marvin's funeral."

"And how is it you propose to do that? You have air fare?" she hissed. "You gonna get your aunty in New York there to pay for it?"

We both knew that was out of the question. Aunty Sylvia wanted nothing to do with my mother, my mother's sister and nothing remotely to do with Guyanese politics. She was not a shy woman about what she would and would not do.

"Celestine, jus relax yourself, gyal!"

"Relax myself? My aunt just got shot and my uncle is dead." Now it was my voice that was getting loud. I heard something knock on the other side of the wall that I shared with Gerty and made an effort to lower my voice.

"You just focus on what you doin there. I just wanted to tell you about your aunt."

"I'm sorry!" I stammered. "I'm sorry for not –."

"Yes, yes whatever. Just don't do it again. Yuh lucky this belt can't reach over to you there."

That made me laugh. And soon she started laughing too.

We laughed just about as loudly as we had been yelling a minute before. Then when we caught our breath I said goodnight before anything else could go wrong. Laying back on my bed, I could not think another single thought.

At breakfast the next day, Caitlyn cut her grapefruit with murderous precision while Gerty stirred around a bowl of oatmeal. We were just another table of hungover girls, traces of eyeliner still visible under puffy eyes, wearing leggings and hoodies and devouring piles of home fries and eggs.

"Guess who I hooked up with last night?" Gerty said into her oatmeal. I rolled my eyes.

She wanted us to say it. Caitlyn obliged.

"Jason. Finally?"

Gerty nodded her head enthusiastically. I never quite understood why "hooking up" was some kind of miraculous achievement. I was confused about what was involved in "hooking up", but too embarrassed to ask. Gerty grinned mischievously.

"It was AMAZING!"

Again, I could not be sure of what exactly was amazing, but thankfully I really didn't want to know. Gerty turned to me.

"I saw you and Richard leaving early. Did you guys, ah, you know, hook up?"

We kissed, but I was sure hooking up was more than that. So I shook my head "no."

"Where did you guys go?" she pressed. But fortunately, at that moment, Jason and his friends walked in, and Gerty forgot about me completely.

"OMG hide me!" Gerty squealed. But instead of hiding she

smoothed over her curly bangs and smacked her lips to re-fresh her lipstick. A little went over her lip, but I did not bother to say anything.

I continued to poke at my eggs until I saw that Richard trailed behind them, talking to Alex, who was unabashedly staring at me, his eyes smiling with knowledge. I knew then that Richard had confided in his friend. I wondered what he had told him? That we kissed? That campus security had found us smoking a joint? That I hadn't spoken to my mother in three weeks? No, he wouldn't say that. I remembered about his mother and realized how selfish I sounded. No, he proba-bly had not mentioned mothers.

Walking across the crowded hall, his haunted loner look took on a darker hue. I thought I saw the loss in him now, maybe I had seen it all along. Something in the way he chewed his lip and scowled after he smiled as if he didn't believe that he was good enough to smile, or had vowed to never smile again.

Soon they were upon us.

Gerty scrolled thoughtlessly on her phone, pretending to send a text message. One of Jason's frat boyfriends, Donny I thought his name was, or maybe Ronny asked,

"Do you guys mind if we sit here?"

Gerty suddenly came to life and greeted all of them. Some of them wore the sports jerseys of school teams. The athletes here were no different from athletes anywhere, arrogant, cocky, and fond of using women like Kleenex. Jason's friend group was a mixture of jocks and economics and business ma-jors and in many cases both. I started thinking of how to get away. As everyone settled into seats, we discovered that we were one chair short.

Richard was the last man standing. I was about to get up and give him my seat, happy to flee the celebration gathering for Jason and Gerty's first hookup, but he refused. Kindly, he said, "No, that's okay, I ate earlier. I have to go to the library" then walked away.

Everyone looked back and forth between us. Caitlyn raised her eyebrows in a scandalous and unkind manner. Some of the boys chuckled. Then they all set about recounting every part of the night. Which parties they all went to at what time and who said what and who couldn't find who last night and where they settled down to order pizza and play video games. After a few minutes had passed, I excused myself, saying that I had to use the bathroom, but I wasn't sure where I was going.

You see, I had been trying all morning not to think about Aunty Zoe and Uncle Marvin. I kept telling myself that I wasn't ready to think about it. That if I waited a little longer, I would be calm. I would be able to process it later. But I kept feeling a phantom gunshot wound. Right where my shoulder meets my chest. It throbbed and I rubbed it absentmindedly. Mostly I did not want to be washed over with fear – I could feel my aunt's fear and her sadness. It was for her that I found myself breathing quickly in the Women's bathroom, crying as loud as I guessed the walls could mask.

I sat on a closed toilet seat, the tears rolling down my cheeks effortlessly. Through my blurred vision, I attempted to read the poster that had been posted inside of the stall:

Student Council Needs You

There were pictures of students dressed up like adults, shaking hands, holding meetings, and shuffling documents. This must be where all the budding corrupt senators started. That had certainly been the case in Guyana. The student government members in my secondary school were the spoiled kids of rich men, government officials themselves.

Aunt Zoe would drag me along to birthday parties and sit-down dinners with the other powerful, political families of Guyana. I remember the delight of watching her sashay into the party in bright floral dresses and heels, Uncle Marvin by her side in a charcoal gray suit and oval-shaped sunglasses just big enough to cover his eyes. The two were a topic of gossip and intrigue; Uncle Marvin. a quiet, no-nonsense kind of man with a powerful presence, and Zoe, long-legged and vivacious, easy to laugh, and easy to cry. But no children. Was there secret unhappiness or was the beautiful Zoe a barren woman? I had never asked.

But I heard the whispers around the snobby teen table where I was usually dropped off by my aunt and ignored or laughed at by my age-mates. Although Aunt Zoe brought me around like I was her daughter, everyone knew that my mother was dirt poor and that my father had left. I was the imposter and the kids were merciless in seeing through my disguise even if the adults pretended not to notice.

I passed many of those warm evenings in itchy dresses and ill-fitting shoes eating finger food and sneaking sips of wine. Being an outcast among the teens, I was left to watch the adults. Uncle Marvin was a natural wonder. He sat in one place and before long it seemed like the whole party was moving in his orbit. He wasn't loud and boisterous like the other MPs, but he had a vision. A vision so powerful that even its whispers could enchant the whole room. He spoke of building a new Guyana, cleaning up the government, and reclaiming the natural resources that should have ensured that every child went to bed with a full belly. He spoke of medical care as if it were a right and not a privilege. Around him, while many eyes were wide with hope, others narrowed with suspicion.

One clear spring night, as we left a retirement party, I found myself walking side by side with Uncle Marvin. Aunt Zoe was chit-chatting for far too long with the hostess.

"How did you like the party, Celestine?" He asked. We never had much to talk about, or rather I was usually too intimidated by him to strike up a conversation.

"It was fine, I guess. I could see you were having a good time. People listen to you."

He stopped abruptly, turning to look me in the eye. I looked everywhere else, spotting my aunt doing a carefree sprint towards us across the lawn. Marvin was still focused on me.

"People might listen to you too if you told us what was going on in that head of yours."

At the time, I had scowled with chagrin. Now, teary-eyed in the girls' bathroom, I tore the student council poster off of the door, reading on.

Learn More About Law & Government Practice Democratic Procedures Work with Others to Create Change Make Your Voice Count

I was curious about this Student Council. I noted the well-placed American flags in the photographs. You couldn't help but feel that this student council was a group that was intent upon true, American democracy. I could almost hear Mr. Bashir whisper the word "democracy" like a wish. We were *supposed* to have democracy in Guyana, but nowhere in the texts of Greek historians was there mention of so many people lying, cheating, stealing, and killing. Had democracy killed Uncle Marvin? Could that be so? Democracy to lead a woman as gentle as Aunt Zoe to suffer a gunshot wound? Does democracy mean that blurred line between order and chaos? I longed to know.

6

He waited three days to text me. I waited one hour to text him back. It was only fair to make him wait a little bit. When we met for our first meeting – no one had said that it was a date, so we started off a bit chilly. In a busy corner of the campus Starbucks we drank coffee as people filed by, looking at us curiously. I did not want to believe they were surprised to see Richard with a Black girl. I suspected that for most it was plain old nosiness and fodder for gossip. We had chatted online for coffee together so many times, but after Cloudy Point, I feared we had gotten to know too much of each other too soon. But then the jokes began.

"You remind me of my daughter!" he croaked in his best impersonation of the security guard.

Back in his room (I wanted to avoid Jason-obsessed Gerty at any cost), he played sad indie rock from fancy-looking speakers. He showed me various pieces of film equipment: a tripod, several cases with different lenses, his old camera that was broken but he couldn't throw away. And of course, he had books, and not just a copy of *The Sun Also Rises* from his freshman lit class. A small bookshelf was filled with volumes on everything from the global economy to biography and history. I smiled to myself. There was something so bracing about a fellow nonfiction reader.

That gave me all the courage I needed to kiss him. And

since that night we kept sneaking around, or at least it felt that way. We kept hiding our faces in the daytime and feeling each other's breath on our bodies at night.

We had not had sex yet, and I did not know why. I was certainly not concerned with saving myself for marriage, I did not find my virginity precious. I think it was the way that we were in public. Sometimes I felt that if I did not wave, he would pass me. He had rejected yet another invitation to sit and eat with us. As he walked away, Caitlyn said "He's kind of an asshole." And as eager as I usually was to counter Caitlyn, I couldn't help but agree.

I had never been of much use in the kitchen, but my mother believed she was a master chef. Occasionally, usually on a Sunday, she would begrudgingly try to teach me how to cook whatever dish she was making.

"Celestine, come here." she would call, the house was small enough that I could find "here" by her voice. Candice was always fervent to cook and clean on Sunday mornings as if to repent for her absence at church.

In bed, I heard the chickens squawking out back. I wondered what they were saying to me and pretended that they were urging me to stay in bed. Mummy came and pulled the sheets from on top of me.

"Celestine wake up, gyal! Don't you know it's already 6:30?" I heard her footsteps slapping against the broken wooden plank floors. On any other day of the week, she did not know 6:30 AM from 12 PM, but on Sunday.

"If you have any hope of finding a man, you better get your ass up and learn to cook dis soup. Come an make the dumplings."

In the kitchen, a tall pot bubbled ominously like some witchcraft stirred in it. My mother kept adding things, eddoe, yam, and plantain, while I rolled lumpy balls of dough.

"This is the best soup in all a Guyana." Candice said with unshakable certainty. The soup was the only thing that I ever really learned how to make. My cook-up rice was always mushy and my roti was not soft, but crisp. Mummy would examine these failed meals with fear and desperation, sure that I would be single until my dying day.

"You mus find yourself a soup-loving man, eh Cele?" she would laugh. I had gathered as many of the ingredients as I could find here on campus, which wasn't much but I still knew how to make misshapen dumplings, peel yams, and chop onions. Although I missed the cassava and most of all the hidden pieces of oxtail that salted the whole soup and hid at the bottom of the pot, with most of the spices and herbs at my disposal, I would still be able to make the soup.

Margo was in sweatpants and a sports bra, splayed on the couch in the living room area which was attached to the kitchen. I listened vaguely to *Real Housewives of New Jersey* as I cut up the ingredients. Caitlyn passed through on the way to her room and stopped to frown at the television.

"This is garbage, Margo." Margo didn't even blink, she was transfixed by the rich, petty housewives.

"This is improv at its finest."

There was nothing more likely to make Caitlyn roll her eyes than Margo's thespian talk. She looked over to see what I was doing, wrinkled up her nose at the smell of the now boiling ingredients. She didn't ask me anything, she didn't want to know.

"I guess I'll just study in the library." Caitlyn spat, looking between the two of us. I would not have surprised to see a drop of drool drip from Margo's mouth and I was focused on making my soup as full-bodied and smelly as possible to drive her away. *Maybe it's true*, I thought, *about white people and spices.*

The International House was holding a South American food festival. The name was much bigger than the actual event. I would bring the best soup from Guyana and I had tried to convince Margo to make something from Venezuela, but she gave me a confused look. I forgot sometimes that she was practically American, or as American as the country would let her be. Her parents had been the immigrants. She was not ashamed of this fact as much as she felt shame for not knowing more of the culture and speaking only passable Spanish. I could tell it hurt for her to think about, and so I didn't bring the food festival up again.

Maybe twenty-something international students and three faculty advisors milled around the living room area while the kitchen was crowded with chefs. Spicy smells wafted over the cozy interior – two couches and a broken recliner, wooden tables with solid wooden seats, heavy, multicolored drapes covered the long windows. A line of flags decorated the walls.

I loved coming to the International House. Four wizened seniors lived there. Nafiza was Palestinian and passionate about social justice issues. Alexi was a dark-haired Bulgarian girl who smoked cigarettes out on the rooftop sometimes at night. She was also a poet. Then there was Helena, a German girl who played the flute beautifully but made little noise otherwise. Then one boy, Robert, was a skinny, dark-skinned Nigerian boy who has been trying to sweet-talk me since I stepped on campus. He was one of those people who are so aggressively happy that it makes you question whether you might be sad. Even when I refused him, his tone was still cheerful: "You are what I'm looking for, Queen. I don't want these skinny white girls!"

I scanned the room now for him and not finding him, I sat down on the corner of one of the plush couches, relieved.

Lucy, the Kenyan girl whose visage I had seen on the way to Cloudy Point with Richard, appeared before me smiling. I jumped a little when I first saw her, remembering.

"Here for the free food?" she grinned, her dark lips parting to reveal pristine teeth. She wore her hair in a puff atop her head the way that I used to back home. The style looked so out of place here. There were not many Black girls and the ones that we had straightened their hair or wore braids as I did. I secretly envied her.

She was tall with skin dark and shiny like a coffee bean. Lucy was a dancer and you could see that she was born for it. With her legs crossed and her back straight, she was elegant in a way that I always hoped to be. She knew how to give you just enough smile to think you might have pleased her, although you could never be quite sure.

"Yes, free food and a break from gossip and drama."

Lucy laughed a kind of slow, lazy laugh and revealed her smile generously.

"Those friends of yours, they must be bored. They make lots of entertainment for themselves."

Her voice was deep and lackadaisical. Every word she spoke sounded like a fortune being told.

"That they are," I said, feeling somewhat embarrassed. This often happened to me around campus, people would comment on what interesting company I kept. They were mostly referring to Gerty, who was known around the school for being boisterous and dramatic, someone that you would perhaps laugh with in the back of the class, but not go on a cross-country road trip with. Or for that matter, live with.

"I hear you're running for office?" She inclined her head.

Rumor sprung from silence in this place, silent listeners, silent watchers, not so silent friends.

"Yes, how did you know?"

"Oh, you know, through the grapevine. Will you be joining the diversity council, or is some other cause calling to you?" Her tone had gone cold, and it was clear which answer I was meant to give.

"Yes, I do hope I'll get a spot on the diversity council."

"You will," she said flatly, "But listen, me and a few of the other dancers have started an African dance club."

"That's great!" A student came around with a tray of pastries. I plucked a delicately made tart the server said was called Empanada de Viento, cheese empanadas sprinkled with sugar, Lucy politely refused.

"I know, thank you. It's just that, well the teacher that we have coming in can't keep coming for free. So, it's not even officially a club yet. They say that if we don't have a faculty liaison, but the professors are the ones who don't have time to teach it."

It was more than I had ever heard Lucy say at once, and when she was done she looked exhausted. I had the sense that she was recharging to say more, so I was quiet.

"Anyway, we need … we need so many things."

"You can't get the budget without being listed as an official organization, you can't get listed as an organization without a faculty member and none of the dance faculty is willing to put forward the time."

"Yes," Lucy nodded enthusiastically, "You're good! So now, what should I do?"

"I…I don't know."

"But you'll see about it right? On the student council?" My mouth was dry with sugar crystals and cheese. I nodded, swallowed my spit, and said, "Yes, definitely!" as if I believed it.

Walking out of International House with the remains of Guyana's best soup sloshing in the big pot I carried with me, I felt determined. I felt that I had been given a mission. I felt a different kind of responsibility. Not responsibility as heavy, back-breaking burden that always seemed to get heavier and heavier like it did in Guyana, but responsibility coupled with power. I did not know what my plan for Student Council was before. Perhaps to just observe, listen and never interact, but when I considered that question, I felt foolish for ever having thought that I could shut up in any setting. Just like that, a new spirit had been unlocked within me. Some translucent being, a glow and a shadow in the night water that had been floating with me all along, breaking the surface and changing form. I wondered how much of me was still hidden.

When I arrived in Richards's room, I set the pot on top of his desk with a bang.

"You want a bowl of soup?" There was something about just saying the word "soup" that made my accent linger all throughout the sentence.

He had been digging through a box of old documents, but Richard looked up and smiled.

"I love the sound of your voice," he muttered, then looked away, embarrassed "Uh... and yes to the soup. Thanks, I'm starving."

I bet Richard Wirth had never starved a day in his life, but I was still happy to feed him.

7

We're headed to Monte Carlo on a boat. The ocean salt sprayed into my eyes, but I would not close them. Looking out into the unending sea, it really did seem possible to go far enough away. Maybe I watched to make sure that no shore crept up. Richard held me by the waist, his sword dripped blood onto the hem of my yellow, satin gown. With his arms around me, I felt as if I understood something for the first time. Not love, but security, the feeling of being wanted and needed. I never thought I had the right to feel so sure. But it was happening – what other evidence could I need? We had passed some kind of barrier now. The barrier between his body and mine.

"Celestine!" He called. *"Celestine!"*

Suddenly I knew that the voice was not Richard's, but that of my professor. The lights were back on and the film credits were rolling on the screen. Professor Chabot, a willowy and wrinkled woman with long white hair and hard dark eyes, was holding the attendance board and calling my name.

"Yes? Yes, Professor?" I answered innocently as if I didn't know what I had done. A few students around me giggled.

Professor Chabot grunted and went on to the next name. She had started taking attendance at the end of class since she never seemed to make it in time. She wasn't the type to really care about a sleeping student, but still, it bothered me that I had fallen asleep in class.

At the end of May, I was not sleeping right.

For one thing, Gerty and Jason had taken to having sex under the mask of loud rap music at night, a technique that definitely was not working, as I heard *both* very clearly.

Even in moments of silence, my mind would not let me rest. I thought about Aunty Zoe all the time, too much of the time. I remembered the feeling of her knees against my shoulder blades when she would plait my hair. Mummy would always have to redo the process later because Aunt Zoe's braids were never tight enough to hold a style. Mummy would blame me for crying while she braided.

"Everybody got a tender head. You tink is just you that feel pain, baby?"

I used to think that the National Library was a palace with its geometric shape and endless windows, its body cloaked in all white. The first time I went to visit Aunt Zoe there I was ten and I didn't know if I was allowed beyond the tall, regal gates, so I stood there and waited for Aunt Zoe to come get me. She laughed when she saw me.

"You mustn't be scared, Celestine. All ah dis is for you." She gestured towards the walls and walls of books, more than I had ever seen before. Books with beaten, threadbare covers, golden lettering fading into their spines. Shelves so tall that they frightened me then, but by the age of seventeen, I leaned on those shelves like an extension of my own spine, taking from them and re-shelving with quiet care.

The way that she danced at parties, sweeping across the dance floor with long legs and dancing with herself better than any of the wining couples around her. *Would she ever dance that way again?* Of course, she would. But now her body had seen pain, her mind had seen pain. So maybe not? The knowledge of pain lingers and decays the body and spirit. I had the first inkling of losing her and it stayed in my every breath.

Sometimes I went to Richard's room in Matterson, enduring the stares of the girls who lived on his hall – makeup-less white girls with their hair in careless top-knots filling their water bottles at the fountain. At least one of them was always there and we never spoke. They just stared, tightlipped, as water overflowed from their water bottles and onto their hands.

He liked to fall asleep with his arms around me, but when I heard his breath grow heavy, my eyes would open. I would stare out of his window, watching the trees dance in the balmy shadows outside. His pale hand, strewn lifeless across my stomach, looked like a mistake. The soft hair of his almost mustache quivered with every long exhale. He slept so sweetly, I envied his sleep. So easy and deep.

Those nights I wondered who I was, wondered if I had been abducted and placed here as a ruse. Wondered if what I felt for Richard was real or just new. Everything here was so new. Every time I slipped into the comfort of the place, studying indulgently on a crisp, green lawn, listening to orchestra concerts or indulging in what they called brunch, something would happen.

Some pop culture reference or unknown dish would remind me that I was alone.

Maybe I was trying to get rid of this "alone". Blow it out

like a flickering candle whose flames wane and dance before it extinguishes.

I handed in my paperwork for Student Council and a few days later I got an official-looking email saying that I had been selected for the council. Only the senior members of the council were subject to student votes. As Lucy had predicted, I made it onto the Diversity Committee. I wanted to tell someone and so I texted Richard, a new phenomenon that I was really enjoying. He sent me little messages, funny messages. Sometimes they were about our history class together, sometimes about events around campus, our days, when we would be where.

":D :D :D I knew you would get it!"

Richard had the book of bylaws and procedures in his room – he had considered running last year – and he told me I could have it if I came to pick it up. He just getting in himself when I arrived at Matterson hall, so together we walked up four flights of stairs to his single room at the end of a long hallway. Under the clinical lights of the dorm, he searched for his room keys long enough for awkwardness to surface. He smiled back at me, handsome and well-meaning as ever.

Finally finding his keys, he pushed the door open and flicked on the light. The room was neat, too neat. But when I saw a sock toe not quite stuffed into his dresser drawer, I could see other little clues around the room that he had made a conscious effort to tidy up. It made me nervous and happy all at once.

"Well, this is it." he said, gesturing around the tiny room, light streaming in through a narrow window over the bed.

"It's nice," I told him, nodding and looking around. He

put on a slow, grey song from a band he said was called Deer Hunter. I did not know what to think of the name – it was so uniquely American. Deer hunting is something that you see in American television and movies.

"You can sit," Richard said, motioning towards the bed. It was the only place to sit. His desk chair was piled high with books.

He searched through a drawer and produced a thick packet fastened with a black clip. It reminded me of my reading for American History class that I would have to tackle some time after this. Whatever this was – the handing over of materials. That's all. But it wasn't all, was it? Since that night at Cloudy Point, we hadn't really gotten a chance to talk alone again. We were only bumping into each other, online for coffee or between classes. Or maybe I had memorized the routes I needed to take to see him and the time that he finally arrived at Starbucks, checking his plain, leather watch compulsively. Through texts we had set up a date for the end of the week, but neither of us had counted on being alone together so soon.

I was wearing shockingly pink workout shorts, my only available option. I hadn't done laundry in a long time, saving my quarters with tact. I needed the money to buy bagels on Sunday and be social, even though I still hadn't gotten over the mystery of bagels. I also needed the money to buy smoothies on Saturday night and for the liquor to wash it down with later.

I was down to my final pair of underwear, my least favorite pair, a hand-me-down from Anika. I could never let myself relax in them. I felt quite foolish accepting the thick packet of pages with my own life in the state that it was. My pure exhaustion was making me manic. I was wired all the time, in the process of being Celestine and making sure that Celestine was being properly consumed by others. It was a stressful business and yet now I was also very eager to transcend consumption, to feed and give on my own terms, naysayers be damned. There was this fire in me that was burning up everything around me, anger I had never called anger because I had been taught only to be nice. The anger must have been born out of exhaustion because it seemed like the old Celestine had tried and tried until she croaked. And the present Celestine, the one I conjure up in the nightwater, who thinks she's too clever and could maybe lead something and influence people. And no matter how dark I was by my mother's estimation or how ugly I was as Anika used to tell me daily, I was beautiful. Yes, I was beginning to feel like the girl I saw in the mirror.

I flipped through the endless pages of rules and procedures. It was a simple unicameral setup with committees, voting, and a president.

"Who is the president?" I realized that I did not know. Richard seemed surprised.

"Jason Feltman."

I realized why he was surprised that I didn't know. That was the same Jason that Gerty had been pursuing with mixed success. Undoubtedly, she had mentioned the fact that he had won the run for Student Council President several times, proud of him as if she were his first lady and not a hookup. My mind had been elsewhere. Aunt Zoe was home from the hospital and I called her nearly every night even though she scolded me for wasting minutes.

The night at Cloudy Point had changed things for me. The last string of control that Gerty had on me was that her future boo, as she optimistically called him, was a distant friend of Richard's. A friend, but distant. Jason's friend and fellow Phi Beta Sigma, Alex was friends with Richard. Gerty wanted the two groups to spend time together and although the effort might have been made at least partially with them in mind, both of us seemed like unwilling participants.

Richard rarely spoke with Alex, so the wire that held us to the equation grew tenuous.

It was common practice – this kind of artificial marriage of social groups for mutual benefit, but the only people who seemed to end up in happy relationships went lone wolf, ditching the pack mentality. But usually, no one was willing to admit to wanting a relationship. The group marriage had served its purpose, at least for me. It had been obvious from the moment that Richard and I were able to break through our awkwardness and speak that groups were no longer a factor. We had other things to talk about besides mutual friends.

I looked at him over the manual. He was watching me read, his black frames perched on the tip of his nose. With one finger, I pushed the frames back. He laughed.

"You look like an old man."

It wasn't just his glasses that made me feel that way. Sometimes when he did not think that anyone saw, his façade fell away. He had a look that was eternally worried, eternally forlorn. I liked this melancholy in his character. It showed he was incomplete like me.

"Are you sure you want to do this?" He leaned back on the bed, but then sat up straight, unsure of how to position himself.

"Yes," I said, flipping to the next chapter on committees.

"It's just, it's not what you might think it is." He faltered, watching me carefully. "Like if you really want to get things done, it's not like that." I laughed.

"No democracy is like that, Richard. At least no modern democracy. This is far from ancient Athens and even that – ,"

"Stop," he said, shaking his head at me. He was in constant disbelief of me. I liked that.

"Don't give me a speech about Ancient Rome."

"Athens."

"Athens. I just don't want you to... What do you want to do there? Eighty percent of the council members are pre-law, rich parents, done with money, looking for power and status. The frats are certainly well represented." He flitted his eyes, hoping that the portrait that he had painted was enough.

"The other twenty percent gets pummeled and the Young Republicans Club pretty much runs the Treasury."

"But there were just new elections..."

"Trust me, you don't get it."

"Richard, I don't like it when people tell me that I 'don't get' something. Especially when I think I get it. You're assuming nothing changes, but then you should think of why nothing ever changes. Are you, in fact, doing something to cause change?"

"I spend my time doing other things."

"So, you've never tried to change anything, but you're sure it's impossible?"

He did not say anything. I stood up, conscious of his eyes on me. I touched an expensive-looking camera on his dresser.

"You spend your time like this?" he nodded.

"Photography?"

"And videography, film..."

Of course, I already knew that. I'd seen him filming once behind the freshman dorms with a fairy-looking blond girl, speaking in hushed lines.

"Take a picture of me now," I said, on a jealous impulse. I looked around the room for a good spot to pose. I stood next to his Smiths poster, stretching my leg onto the chipped radiator for effect. I laughed. It felt like it was a sexy thing to do. I threw my head back, a bold pose to rival even that pale, beautiful girl's sadness.

Richard stood up, reaching instinctively for the camera. From the way that he carefully took it out of the case and adjusted the lens just so, you could tell that he knew the chic black Nikon intimately. Loved it, even.

He took a few of me like this, in my gym shorts. I liked to watch his mouth screw up beneath the camera. His lips looked as sweet as the cherry candies on the dish by Aunty Sylvia's front door. I swallowed my spit and thought of cherry candies. When he moved the camera away from his face, he was still staring at me just as intently as I was sure he had been behind the lens. "Do something else now."

"What?"

"Something unexpected."

I wanted to play along. My hands went to parts of me that I always unburdened first when I closed my bedroom door at night. When I was finally alone. I took down my hair from its neat bun, running my fingers through the length of it. At first, I did not want to look at him, but slowly I turned my face upwards and saw him. It was too late to be ashamed of the protruding kinks at the roots or to lament how not-quite-white-girl-straight it was.

He put the camera up to his face as I shook my hair out, but I didn't hear a snap.

"You're so…" he began, lowering the camera.

"Beautiful?" I suggested. "It's the only way I like the rest of your sentence."

He chuckled, "I was gonna say 'honest'."

I'm so honest, I thought to myself, not knowing if I really liked the sound of it. My throat clenched and my eyes kept moving to different parts of him. His legs, so pale with sandy covering of hair, his forearms taut with his camera in hand. There was something comical in my attraction to him. It seemed as if it shouldn't be so.

He put the camera down on his dresser and I went to him. We kissed as if wishing that our lips had never been parted. On the bed, our bodies felt new together, awkwardly our own but desperate to connect. His hands hesitated, moving up my waist, but I held them there against me, utterly fascinated with every twinge and flutter of his body.

Richard sat up and turned to me. His hair was tousled, his breathing still heavy and fast.

"Let's go to dinner."

"You're hungry?" I asked incredulously.

"I'm… well, yes," The flush, which before had only reddened his cheeks enveloped his ears as well. "I want to take you to dinner." he finished.

"You're kidding."

"No, we're going to dinner." He kissed me again, quickly as if he didn't trust himself. I closed the student government manual. A few of the pages had been creased by the weight of our bodies. The fact that the book bore the first damage of us somehow endeared it to me. Everything that we discussed, the pointlessness of student council, his binding commitment to photography – a soft glow lay over it all as if we had culti-vated rose-colored energy, a foretold healthy future.

By my second trip to his room, we had kissed again. I let his hands roam up my thigh and touch over my cotton panties. Maybe I would have stopped him if I hadn't been so taken aback by the longing and command in his touch. I thought about Kelvin in Guyana for a flash, the way that he touched me like he didn't know what he was feeling for. This was not that. And perhaps because it was so different, I found myself wanting more.

I rubbed his thigh the way that he rubbed mine, stroked my fingers up the stiffness in his khaki pants. What I felt was not lust, more like a genuine curiosity about his body. I wanted to see more Richard – what kind of belly button he had and how much or how little chest hair, what he tasted like... I imagined a cool, fresh taste like a cucumber. And maybe it was the image of a cucumber that made me unzip his pants, pulling them down to his knees like I'd seen in the movies.

Anika had once told me what to do.

"It's no big deal. Just open up so..." She had opened her mouth like a wide and perfect "o". "An yah suck it down like a mango seed." She winked.

He wore green and white striped boxer shorts. Then he unzipped my skirt and it became a race. He unbuttoned his shirt and pulled a crisp, white undershirt up over his head. I took off my t-shirt and let him see me in my bra – an old-fashioned, thick strapped, and lacy undergarment of my Aunty Sylvia's choosing. I was too afraid of what he would think of my breasts to be embarrassed about the bra, though. Had he ever seen a black girl's breasts before? Maybe online, but I didn't want to think about him watching porn. And I wasn't sure that they were big enough either or if my nipples were the right color. I decided to leave my bra on. He was all pink and pale and covered in light brown hair. He wound his arms around my waist and kissed my stomach.

"It's my first time... doing anything."

He seemed surprised. "Anything?"

I nodded. It was not worth mentioning the dry humping that Kelvin had initiated once, or the touches that we had given each other when our eyes were dim with liquor.

"Wow. I thought..."

"You thought wrong." I smiled at this, desperate to have something to lighten the awkwardness.

"But you, you want to? Do it?"

"Have sex?"

He nodded solemnly, his hands moving to cover his privates.

I pushed his hands away. "I've already seen it. Why cover up now?" I held him and stroked him up and down as Richard's face went red and his pretty, green eyes glossed over, unseeing. He was nothing like a mango seed; certainly not as sweet. But I liked the taste of the salt on his skin.

First, he used his hands, rubbing my body up and down carefully. I giggled as his hands went over my ticklish tummy and held my breath when his hands cupped my covered breasts pinching the fabric over my nipples. By the time his hands found my back, I was used to their warmth and unexpectedly roughness. When he came to my bra, he asked if he could take it off. I nodded, unable to imagine myself articulating a reason to keep it on. I could not stop thinking about the fact that another human being was inside of me and I kept thinking about what that meant, unable to find satisfactory answers. I held on to him for dear life because it felt that way, like he was holding me over some great precipice.

8

Pure white light poured in through the window the third Thursday in November. Aunt Sylvia said that she would be working on Thanksgiving and that I should not bother to come back to New York, but truthfully, I was more excited about the blizzard that was meant to hit the Midwest than a dubious holiday that as far as I could tell was mostly about eating. I found it curious how rarely people spoke about the history behind the holiday. As far as my history books told, the relations between the natives and the white settlers was strained at best and bloody at worst, but most people only talked about turkey. Last year I had gone to Brooklyn to be with Aunty Sylvia who only had the morning off and left me to microwave cold curry. Turkey curry, she was not heartless.

I ran to the window and peered out at the vast campus blanketed in heavy, white snow. I had the room to myself since Margo had gone to visit family in Florida for the short break. Whereas the night before I had felt giddy with freedom strutting around the room naked, I now felt isolated, a tropical Black girl caught in an immense snow drift. As I sank back into bed, I heard a knock at the door. Most of the campus had gone home to their families, and there were only a few other people who I knew that had opted to stay. Sure enough,

Richard was on the other side of the door, holding a steaming bag of hot breakfast items.

We set up a breakfast table at my desk.

"So, you really stayed?"

"I really did."

"What about your dad?"

Richard cracked open a bottle of orange juice in response and drank deeply.

"You ever had a snowball fight?" Ignoring my question, Richard proceeded to bundle me in sweaters and hats and two pairs of socks.

"You really don't have the wardrobe for this do you?" He smirked. Outside my eyes were nearly blinded by white. Snowflakes still whipped around, pelting at my cheeks like tiny daggers. My feet sunk into the crisp, wet tundra until only my knees could be seen moving through. Richard was in a thick, puffy coat, suited for a veteran explorer. He picked me up, and wrapped my legs around his waist and my hands around his shoulders. He took two more steps and yelped as we both fell forward into the snow. He showed me how to make a snow angel.

And we made a trip to the coffee shop, which was empty but for the two of us.

We were moving so slowly that we found ourselves exhausted as we reached the back of the maintenance building where a soft hill saw into dense forest. The trees were heavy with snow. The snow was so white under the glaring November sun. The snow promised to melt quickly, but for now everything was perfectly white, perfectly smooth. And bulky as I was underneath my mismatched scarves and sweaters, I ran up the hill until I was swimming in snow. When I got to the top, I was frosted and drenched.

"You have to come up here!" I shouted to Richard. He was shaking his head and laughing at me. His cheeks and his ears were red. It always worried me, how red he got, I wondered if an earlobe might fall off, but eventually I wrote it off as one of the strange wonders of white people. "C'mon what are you tired?" We were both incredibly tired, but Richard thrived on his need for 24/7 Redbull fueled alertness. He spent time shooting and editing when he wasn't studying. Any schedule that required 8 hours of sleep was out of the question. He hated tired, so he struggled up the hill as quickly as the deep snow would allow and dusted off a rock that we shared although both of our butts couldn't fit on it comfortably. The snow was melting though my jeans, through my leggings.

"My ass is so cold on this rock." I said. He turned half way around, picked me up and put me on his lap, scooching back so that he then sat comfortably.

"Someone's feeling passionate!" I laughed.

"Something like that." His voice drifted off. He was looking at me like he'd already lost me. We both knew, I think, that love was not supposed to feel tragic or doomed.

"If only you could hold me this way when the other 98% of the campus was here." He frowned. Why couldn't I manage to stop making Richard frown? He was so much more agreeable when I didn't ask questions. But then there I would go, again and again with the questions. Why not concentrate on how sturdy his arms felt, of how whatever kind of heatwave was coming from his crotch was sure keeping my ass warm. Briefly wondering... is it hard? I squirmed in his lap to see. He seemed both pleased and agitated by my movement. I felt my answer, but his face said something else.

"I don't like PDAs Celestine."

"It's not a secret, Richard. It's like you're the only one who doesn't know sometimes. You ignore me when you want to ignore me, love me in other moments." The words hung in the clear, crisp air.

"Celestine Samuels?"

"Yes?"

He grinned.

"What is it?"

Richard didn't blink looking down at me, I liked to watch his eyelashes and wonder at them – they were long for a boy. Hope awakened within me for the first time. I did not know what he was thinking, only that he seemed to be thinking furiously or his mind had gone blank.

He bent down and kissed me, his lips tasting sweet like the peppermint coffee he had downed earlier. I drank in the warmth of his mouth willingly, a taste my own bitter medicine.

9

He had two cuts through his right eyebrow like he was some kind of thug. Though it was clear that no knife had ever touched him, but he had come to believe it was cool to look as if one did.

Don was a big man — there was no mistaking him for a boy — with the blasé air of a well-oiled player. I wanted to get up almost as soon as I saw him watching me with a lazy grin.

Why did he have to be my partner? They would all be suspicious of us, doubtful of what these two Black kids could do. And I doubted us too. He pulled out a bright green folder with the football team crest emboldened on the cover. I could not say I was surprised.

"Well, little lady, you have any ideas to start?" I could tell he was patronizing me, but I decided to ignore it.

"Yes, actually. I was just looking over the budget for the academic year — a little bit tight isn't it? It seems like this committee has only added three new items to the agenda since it's conception," I scanned the page of notes I had put together, "five years ago... there's only been a diversity committee for five years?"

Don shifted in his seat uncomfortably.

"I guess so."

"Have there only been people of color here for five years?"
"No." he said too quickly.

"So the administration has only started caring in the last five years?" Don narrowed his eyes.

"I wonder how long you'll last here. Your type doesn't usually last in student council. Let me guess, you're dissatisfied, right?"

He folded his hands on the table, big, catcher's mitt sized hands. Dark brown so that even their pale undersides were colored with melanin.

"How could I be satisfied with this pathetic budget? Are you?"

He sighed loudly. "I mean... yeah. Look, all the BSU needs is snack money for meetings. We have that. And our own lounge, which is more than most organizations get." A phrase floated to the top of my consciousness, probably from a text book, *ten acres and a mule.*

"What about other multicultural organizations? Like the international club? Don't they need more funding?"

"Again, funding for what?"

"Funding for events, initiatives, you know, actually making sure that these organizations are active in the Simon College community?"

It was six-thirty then, time for the committees to assemble again and vote on leftover business from the previous school year.

Don got up slowly like a weary, old man. He rubbed his fresh fade forward.

Shuffling the papers that I was sure he'd only brought for show he said, "You're not gonna like it here." He smiled his greasy smile again, then made his way towards the main assembly room. I could see him tall and Black amongst fair hair and pale skin.

I sauntered into the meeting room last and sat at the table in the very back next to a girl that I recognized as one of Margo's theater friends. Come to think of it, it was THE theater friend. The one that Margo whispered about to me in the dining hall.

"I can't stop staring at her… Is it just me or is she, like, unusually beautiful?"

At the time I had dryly said, "It's just you." But now I looked over at the girl's face – big, smiling brown eyes, a wide mouth coated in wine-colored lipstick. Her hair was fiery red, cut short, and tapered. I could see the smooth streaks where she pushed her bracelet-clad hand through with mousse in the morning. She was wearing an ill-fitting pencil skirt, a wrinkled blouse, and chunky, black Doc Martins.

I could not help but smile and think that Margo would approve. She caught me staring and smiled back.

"Hey, you're Celestine, right? Margo's friend?"

Did I sense a hint of embarrassment when she said Margo's name? Maybe I just wanted my friend to be happy.

"Yes, that's right."

"I'm Patty."

Somehow the name fit her. All around us, people were milling around, trying to find their seats, little placards had been placed around the room with our names in alphabetical order. I wondered why committees didn't sit together, not that I wanted to sit next to Don, who was currently whooping it up with a couple of equally beefy men in the front of the room. "What committee are you on?" I asked Patty, who was taking out a fresh notepad. I like a girl with a notepad, I was reminded to take mine out as well.

"Community Relations and Service."

I did not know what that meant exactly, but I knew that I would want to work with her in the future.

Two young men walked in looking very dapper – full gray suits as if they were meeting with a major corporation. They strutted to the front, and it was only when they sat down that I saw that the first man was Jason. He was smiling wistfully as if he had already somehow saved the day just by being here. I chuckled a little to myself. If I blew into his left ear I could whistle out of the right. A few girls had gotten up immediately to greet him. So, I would tell Margo that Patty became flustered at her name, and I would probably say nothing to Gerty about Jason. Or maybe that he was there and in a suit.

"Ugh, they look like *supreme* douchebags," Patty whispered from behind. I nodded in agreement. I took a closer look at the other one and realized that it was Alex. Just about every-ones' ex was on the student council. After strutting to his seat, all of Alex's bravado was gone. His shoulders caved in, and he broodingly stared at his phone beneath the desk.

"Can you believe he's the freaking president?" Patty grum-bled quietly. "Yeah, well, "We The People" voted and as usual, it was just a popularity contest. Some fratboy asshole always ends up winning. And they always bring some obnoxious crony with them."

Alex stood out among the eager looking, document flip-ping, note scratching students around him. I could see his Star Wars socks beneath his too-short dress pants.

"You mean Alex? I thought ..."

"He's never been on the council before so he can't run for president but he can be selected as a vice president."

I hadn't read that part of the guidebook so closely since I did not plan on running for any of the higher positions.

"Welcome to Hell." Patty muttered under her breath. After the meeting, I set off to Rat House to meet Gerty, who had been entreating me through constant texts to read over her African Colonialism paper for her. To be fair, Gerty begged me to read all of her essays. We had learned early on during nervous study sessions our academic weaknesses and strengths. Gerty was a visual learner, which was difficult for her as a history major. She was drawn towards maps of migrations, sketches, and paintings. She should have been an art history major, but she liked the dusty prestige of the History department, which was apparently highly acclaimed in the region. She loved to play the pretend intellectual while chatting utter bullshit with obscure references to historical speeches that she watched on YouTube. She was all about the discussions although many of her conjectures left a stunned silence over the classroom, then a nervous chatter until the professor called on someone else. Her impassioned speech about how she thought that Hitler was still alive and in hiding definitely left an unsettling silence in the classroom. But when it came to writing her theories that almost never really fit the parameters of the assignment, she had no confidence.

The door to Rat House was open. The living room was dark, so I headed up the stairs towards Gerty's bedroom. She was not in the room, so I sat on her bed. Gerty's bedroom was set up in nearly the same way as it was in the old room.

Her walls were plastered with large posters – of course the quintessential Beatles crossing Abbey Road, and Bob Marley smoking a joint washed all in Jamaican colors, but also a few obscure art prints and posters of bands from her hometown of Pittsburgh. The bands had names like Poisoned Boys Die and The Dragon Slayers.

I tried to imagine what she must have been like in high school when she went to see these bands, red streaks dyed into her light brown hair, perhaps wearing a choker or chunky black shoes.

In between the posters there were pictures of her and her friends from back home. She looked equally drunk in all of them, but happy. No one could ever accuse Gerty of not choosing happy. I stood up and walked over to her dresser, observing her endless collection of bracelets and baubles. Gerty was obsessed with little things, anything small and delicate. Simple flower pendants, various small, but beautiful stones that she collected from around campus and pins for her backpack with various pictures, symbols, and sayings. I looked up into the mirror, lamenting my coily roots that wouldn't let the straight hair sit quite flat enough. I thought back to Lucy's natural hair, it really did look nice on her, but that was her. As I smoothed my hair from the middle part down, I heard a noise. It was an unusual noise. Before I could even think of what it was, it made my skin crawl, made my insides go cold. The sound was coming from outside of Gerty's room, that much I knew for sure. And as I approached the hall, I was almost sure of what it was – retching. On panicked instinct, I knocked on the bathroom door.

"Hello? Are you okay?" I asked the peeling green paint of the door.

"I'm fine, leave me alone!" Caitlyn barked, her voice hoarse.

"Are you sick? I can go get medicine."

"I said, 'I'm fine'. What part of that don't you get?"

Numbly, I walked back into Gerty's room. No longer in the mood to preen myself in the mirror, I sat on her bed and watched the campus go by through her window. About a minute later, Caitlyn walked into Gerty's room.

"Do you know when she is due back?" I asked, before she could speak a word. "What are you even doing here? How did you get in here?" She was breathing the way she did when she was about to blow up, filling up the entirety of her frail, narrow chest with breath and huffing and puffing as her face grew red.

"The front door was open."

Caitlyn blinked once hard, annoyed.

"Listen, I'm fine. I just had something at lunch, I don't think the chicken was cooked right."

And at this moment, I wanted to stop her talking and embrace her, because I could not even remember the last time I had seen Caitlyn eat a piece of chicken. But I knew what I was supposed to do, play dumb, buy it.

So I said, "Oh, yes I thought that chicken looked funny." I wished that my words were true, it would help them go down easier.

Once she understood that I would keep her secret, she became visibly more relaxed, a little of her snobbish swagger even came back.

"So, what's up with you and Richard?" To Caitlyn and Gerty, Richard was *the* most interesting thing about me.

"I don't know what you mean." I said pleasantly.

"Are things official?" Gerty had asked me this as well. I found the question nauseating.

"No, I don't know if that's what I... It's whatever. It's not a big deal, we're just..."

"I dunno, Celestine. Maybe you're barking up the wrong tree."

I refused to think of myself as barking. I felt the sympathy for Caitlyn drying and splitting like a nut roasted over a fire. But I had to ask.

"What do you mean?"

"I mean, you're on student council with Don Bradford. I mean, most girls say he's pretty hot and you never know, maybe he'll think you're cute too," She laughed with a hollow, "Get yourself a black guy, you know?" She continued laughing to herself. The words bubbled up like bile at the back of my throat.

"So, I guess your stomach is feeling better?" Caitlyn's face grew drawn.

Thankfully, just then I heard the front door and Gerty's loud and penetrating voice as she spoke to someone over the phone. Caitlyn crossed her arms and turned to leave the room, bumping into Gerty on her way out.

"What the fuck? Are you all having some kind of orgy in my bedroom and you didn't even tell me about it? All of my panties better still be in the drawer! No, not you, mom, I'm talking to Caitlyn and Celestine."

She placed the receiver on her chest. "Mom says 'Hi!'. Say

hi!" She held the receiver out and Caitlyn and I exchanged wary looks before we attempted a joined and mangled "Hi, Mrs. Allen." Caitlyn left promptly, pounding down the steps and out of the door.

Gerty finished up her conversation with her mom, then she showed me her essay outline and a draft that she had put together. I let history carry my mind away.

10

I was beginning to look forward to student council meetings. They gave interesting insights about the inner workings of the college. What progressive initiative could possibly win the favor of the trustees and had real admissions catalogue potential? There were a lot of long winded, sputtering speeches from Jason and tedious debates about trays in the dining hall. Meanwhile I tried to create a proposal for an increase in the diversity council budget. If the proposal were accepted, the item would be added to the agenda, and would perhaps be discussed by the last week of May, a few days before the council adjourned for the summer.

Don sat back during meetings, playing with his pen, listening to his ipod with an earbud in one ear, checking his phone, and laughing at text messages. Every time I asked for his input, he rolled his eyes and gave a useless answer. I had already made the mistake of asking him about formatting the proposal.

"Why are you doing this? Just chill."

"Just chill?"

Talking to him was difficult, my throat grew tight. "The African dance club wants to hire a workshop leader. I want it to be in the budget. And the South Asian society wants to go to a festival in Chicago this spring ..."

"How come no one has come to me with these demands?"

"Maybe because you're such a ..."

He raised his well-groomed eyebrows waiting on my next word.

"Dick. You're such a dick." The room had gone quiet and a few other council members looked over with interest.

Don smiled his slow, sleazy smile. He made his milk chocolate brown eyes twinkle, a look that he probably thought was a panty-dropper. I felt my cheeks growing warm, embarrassed.

After that, I was determined to write the proposal on my own. It meant that I sometimes had to wake up very early after studying into the wee hours of the morning, but I did it. Early one Friday morning, I printed out four copies to be evaluated by the President, Vice President, Secretary and one of the college trustees. I handed the documents to Jason, who was sitting with his frat brothers at a long, wooden table in the dining hall. They all looked up, confused, as I approached.

"Good morning!" I said through a teeth-clenching smile. I passed him the four navy portfolio folders in which I had placed the proposals. He just stared at them on the table as if I had slammed down a flopping fish before him. I could feel all of their eyes on me.

"Hey, Celestine. What's this?" he asked, his good nature was jovial enough, but thin.

"The proposals that I told you about for the Diversity Committee." I was still trying to smile sweetly.

"Oh, you got that done so quickly." he said, his brow furrowing in confusion, a face that Gerty liked to call his "lost puppy face".

"Yes, well the deadline to submit proposals is Friday, right? And the agenda's almost full so, I found a way."

He nodded, his eyes still cold and blank blue even as his lips smiled. "Cool, cool."

He started to turn away and his friends too turned back to their breakfast.

"So when can I expect an answer?"

He turned back around, his face registering a mixture of surprise and annoyance. Alex, who had been scowling beside Jason the whole time, decided to speak up.

"It takes 2-3 weeks. You'll get an email. Does Don know about this?" I felt my own annoyance bubbling over at his last question. I'm sure it showed on my face.

"2-3 weeks you say? Okay, I'll look out for the email."

As I turned away I heard the boys whispering and laughing amongst themselves, but I had already learned that it really did no good to listen to whispering boys. They rarely had anything intelligent to say and I needed to get to the post office before my shift at the Provost's office.

I had started something a little while ago, a letter that first started as a silly note in my journal, but which I added to little by little when I was bored in class or tired of studying. A letter to my father had grown to span four of my tiny journal pages. I ripped them out the night before and tucked them in an envelope along with a full length photo of me – one that Richard had taken outside of my dorm one Saturday morning. I couldn't decide what to put after "dear", so I didn't write "dear" at all, I just started talking. I had come to the conclusion that I would probably graduate before I could save enough to go home and search for him, but it didn't stop me from picking up three extra hours a week at the office, the most that the dowdy, white haired woman would allow.

Beyond wanting to see my father, it was hard to live with the fact that I was bound to this campus. I couldn't run home if I wanted to and I realized that this was the way that it was supposed to be. One gives themselves to America, throws their whole selves into the country with the hope that it will not swallow you alive. I was not meant to go back. My mother had cried tears into my hair because I was not meant to come back, I was not even meant to want to return. America was to soothe all of my desires. If it didn't, then that was my problem, there was something wrong with me.

One day I stopped by the African dance workshop, curious to see what it was all about. The dance studio was hidden behind Miller Theater, a kind of hastily made addendum. There were not many dance students and they used the space wisely with a decent sized auditorium and a few private studios. It was in the first of those studios that I heard the sound of drums emanating from. When I peeked through the glass door, I was disappointed to see that it was only playing from an ipod in the corner. After this initial disappointment, my attention went to the group of four Black girls and an older Black woman with salt and pepper locs. I recognized the girls from around campus, Black girls like me. And yet we still felt like strangers, exercising our God given right to not be friends with someone just because they share the same affliction. But here, now I could see it was a gift to be shared. Their knees touched. Some wore leotards, other wore sweatpants or leggings. All of their eyes were set upon the salt and pepper locs lady who was speaking, and I found my own eyes drawn to her as well. And as if sensing my presence, she turned her head towards the door. Her skin was yellow brown like perfectly baked bread, her eyes squinted as she smiled at me.

"Come on in!" she called.

Lucy looked up and smiled at me. It was odd. To walk into a room and be so welcome.

"Pop a squat," The older woman said. I sat with them. "My name is Saffiya." She spoke warmly, her name sounded sweet and rich like poetry in her even tone. "Now, like I was saying. Next week is going to be the last time that we can meet up, girls. I'm sorry. I've just accepted a position in Boston. It's just the right move for me right now." We were all quiet.

"But Celestine put together the proposal like we talked about, remember?" said Lucy.

Everyone stared at me.

"I did. I just handed in the paperwork this morning. I don't see why it wouldn't go through."

"If it did go through, when would that money be allotted?" The older woman asked.

"Wait a minute. Diversity Committee? Like the people who get the chips for the Black Student Union meetings?" Asked the girl beside me, a sophomore named Naomi. I ignored her.

"You probably wouldn't have the funding until next school year." I said solemnly. Processing everything that had just been discussed, I realized that instead of being a welcomed and unexpected guest I was actually the bearer of bad news.

"Well, there it is." Said another girl, Pamela, a science major rarely seen outside of the lab.

"Hold on! No!" I heard myself saying.

The girl to Lucy's right, Janelle, kissed her teeth. I almost smiled, for the sound reminded me of my mother, but Janelle was annoyed.

"You know the diversity council don't do shit right?" Janelle had a southern drawl that cut between all of the tension. Her eyes locked on mine, challenging me.

"It can. I promise."

"Girl, don't make promises you can't keep."

"I'm going to keep my promises. I don't make promises that I can't keep."

"It shouldn't be that hard to raise some money in the meanwhile and then I can work on trying to get it moved up in the agenda."

Janelle laughed. She was a beautiful woman, her skin was dark and smooth and luminous, her eyelids hung low and her mouth was painted with deep red lipstick.

"You don't get it. The agenda don't give a fuck about your Black ass. My Black ass, *none* of our Black asses." Her voice vibrated off of the mirrored walls and the smooth wooden floor.

"We could raise the money." I said desperately.

"How?" Janelle retorted, "What you want us to have a bake sale, sell some Black girl magic brownies? How much would that bring in? Be real." She stood up suddenly, stretching and bowing forward so that her fingers met her toes. Soon the other girls began to stand as well, sensing hopelessness in my silence, and they were all stretching in a circle.

Saffiya stood up as well.

"You're right, Janelle. We need to start practice. We only have forty-five minutes until the tap girls come looking for this room." I moved to go.

"No, stay Celestine! Don't you want to see what you're fighting for?" Saffiya entreated. I could not bring myself to deny her. With her easy confidence, one could not help but follow her lead.

Saffiya turned on a small radio and a rhythmic beat patterned with drumming filled the room. The girls began to switch their hips as a sonorous voice began to wail in Swahili. I could almost see the awkwardness lifting from their bodies, see them become unburdened and free. They were used to each other. They moved in sync and stretching their spines tall, upwards, as if they were worthy of light, worthy of the sun and all its glory. Saffiya had her eyes closed the whole time. She danced as if her limbs had been born with this knowledge – how deeply the knees should bend and the angles at which she should roll her hips. But aside from her, it was clear that Janelle was the prodigy of the group. Her every move carried certainty that the other girls could only grasp intermittently throughout the performance. Her hips kept moving even after the song had stopped. I spoke before I really thought.

"You all should perform! We could charge for the tickets. Would that keep you for a little while, Saffiya?" The wizened woman smiled slowly in between sips from a water bottle.

"What do you think, girls? Are we ready?"

"Of course we are." Janelle responded immediately. Only after she spoke did she seem to regret agreeing with my idea.

"Hell yes!" Lucy called enthusiastically.

Naomi and Pamela exchanged worried looks.

"I'm not sure," Pamela sputtered, "We're only just learning." Naomi nodded in silence.

"Pamela, Naomi, have you girls ever seen yourself dance? You have nothing to worry about!

We'll practice!" Saffiya assured them.

"Don't be tryna act like you're a good girl, Pam. I see you Saturday nights. You already puttin in practice!" Janelle bent over and started twerking. The girls started laughing and Lucy started singing a Soulja Boy song. Biting her lip, Pamela smiled and started her own kind of slow booty pop. The room was filled with the sound of Black girl giggles, light and translucent like freshly blown bubbles.

11

Let she stay dere.

Apparently that's what Aunty Sylvia had told Candice. I could hear the old woman's

voice,

"She makin money deh, you know. She a work in one of dem office in da school. Let she stay dere."

But the provost's office was only opened through late May; long enough to wrap up graduation. Then it closed for two months and reopened in late summer for the new semester. So eventually, Sylvia conceded and bought me a bus ticket for the day after the office closed. It was a thirteen-hour drive through hills and flat plains. I had made this trip once before on my way from New York to Indiana, but it took me by surprise yet again. The vastness of America was overwhelming. All the roads were like an unending optical illusion, crossing each other and sighing on and on. To either side of me, farmlands sprawled, silos stood like beacons and wisps of towns rose out of the inherently industrious American soil. You would think that a place with so much land would be brimming with opportunity, but it did not look like it. You could see it in the eyes of the people, white people with faces as weathered as the houses whose porches they manned, houses that had belonged to their granddaddy's granddaddy. The closer to New York we got, the more congested the landscape grew and the thicker the air.

Aunty Sylvia was working that day. She was a nanny and the children's parents had gone on vacation to Antigua. She told me to take the 2 or 3 train to Eastern Parkway and that I would find the key to the house underneath the welcome mat. I tried to push my five-dollar bill into the Metrocard machine but it would not take, the machine kept spitting it out.

"Can you hurry the fuck up?" Spat a woman behind me. She sized me up through eyelined eyes, tossing her head of highlighted curls to one side.

"You not from here are you?" She smiled thinly, flipped my five-dollar bill face up and re-entered it. I took my Metrocard and thanked her, although she said nothing in response. I stayed towards the center of the platform, afraid to venture near the yellow lines. I'd never seen so many different kinds of people in one place, milling through, eyes down, books out, headphones in, numb and apart and yet one throbbing mass. I watched the rats dance across the subway tracks, wondering how one could comfortably live in such continuous peril. The train came, kicking up the stale air, I found myself being pushed by strange bodies into the middle of the car and I held for dear life onto a free space on a pole.

By the time I got to Aunty Sylvia's house, I was exhausted. I found myself missing the bed I had left behind in the brick and ivy house I shared with Gerty, Margo and Caitlyn. Aunty Slyvia's house was like a tease. It smelled of the soft and pungent spices of my mother's house in Guyana, it stunk sweetly of dried orange skins and brittle flowers. And yet when I climbed out onto the rickety fire escape attached to the back of the brownstone, I saw that this place was something else.

Brooklyn was teeming with people; different people speaking different languages, dressed in various garbs and carving spaces for themselves. That summer I made friends with the shy young woman from Ecuador who sold snow-cones down Sterling street most summer afternoons. She sold blue and red and white ices from giant industrial tubs, but she had one other tub, a smaller one that looked more like Tupperware hidden in the corner of her cart.

"What's that one there?" I asked, pointing to the tub. Color rose in her cheeks as if I had embarrassed her and she smiled shyly. She had very straight, beautiful teeth.

"Mango. It's homemade. You want to try?" she said very quickly, before she could lose her nerve. All summer, Aunty Sylvia scolded me when she saw the flimsy white paper cups in the garbage.

"It's so you spending yah money, eh? On sweet an ting? You need to take yuhself out of this house and get a little job or so. Because I don't want to hear yah need money for this, money for that. An come Christmas time, yah gon have to pay for your own bus ticket, yah understand me?"

I set up in the little bedroom upstairs, and created towers of books that I had found in the library from my syllabi for next semester. A book with "Dark Continent" in the title that I knew I would either love or hate, a bunch of dense looking books about the War of 1812 which I figured I should start reading now, while I had time to think and concentrate. I picked up a copy of the Bluest Eye. I had never read anything by Toni Morrison before.

I had become thankful for the time away from campus. Idle time in which I could think and think and try to regroup. Most times on campus I could not find the nightwater and when I did, it felt empty and icy, as if it knew that I had abandoned it somehow, perhaps it was a phase that I had now outgrown, a space too cramped for my newly Americanized life to fit. It had all been so simple in Guyana, well, it hadn't really, but I had the same loneliness and longing for all my life. I knew it's contours and what would soothe slaps and lashes and Black and ugly. I didn't know how to soothe the quiet ways I had changed over the last year. The wounds that I felt but could not articulate had changed me and I didn't know how to calm this new girl.

In the kid-sized bed of my Aunty's house, I was able to remember a little bit of myself. Aunty Sylvia always had her ear out for odd jobs that I could do, so when a friend of her employer asked if she knew anyone who could do a quick weekend baby babysitting job for the tidy sum of $500, she told them about me.

The apartment was the size of a house and facing the park on the upper east side. A woman looked at me suspiciously as she held the door for me on the way into the building.

"I'm the nanny." I said almost automatically. Then on the whole way up in the elevator, I was angry with myself.

I smiled benignly at Mr. and Mrs. Connors. Mr. Connors was tall with dark, meticulously close-trimmed hair. He stared at me in a kind of distant, appraising way that made me avoid his eyes. Mrs. Connors kept touching me on my shoulders and giving me encouraging arm pinches. She showed me around their home, bright red hair fluttering in a trail behind her. She introduced me to the children; one was a little baby girl and the other was a five-year-old boy with long, brown hair and huge brown eyes. Caleb, I would learn, was a kind of quiet rebel and Katelyn was as sweet a baby girl as ever there was. Caleb liked to lie about everything from homework to his bedtime. Katelyn cooed serenely in her crib and would settle for a mere whine for food or to be changed. I had never taken care of a baby before, but by the end of the weekend, I felt I knew how. It took intuitiveness and patience.

Ironically, as I changed Katelyn's diaper for the fourth time on the Sunday, Caitlyn from Simon called me. Gerty had sent some funny videos over Facebook – stuff she thought would make me laugh. Margo called me almost every day. She had stayed on campus to do a summer theater program and she was falling in love with her crush Patty. But I hadn't expected to really hear anything from Caitlyn.

"I just wanted to invite you to my family's house on Cape Cod the weekend before school starts. I invited Margo and Gerty too. It'll be fun."

There were voices in the background and she kept growling "I'm coming! In a minute!" in response. She was glad when I said that I had to go, for baby Katelyn had started fussing. I was growing fond of the glassy-eyed baby who didn't have a thought in her mind to use against me. I couldn't help but think of how many foreign, brown faces would watch over her through the years, make her neat sandwiches after her piano lessons and before SAT tutoring.

Richard was in Chicago. He called it "staying with his dad" instead of going home as if there were another place where he really belonged. I envied the brazen way that my white classmates threw away their parents. Try as I might to forget about my mother, I felt as if she would have me by the ear for the rest of my life. No slick remark mumbled too quietly for her retribution and reproach. It felt as if she watched over me like a specter at school, judging what I wore, and what I ate, and how much I drank.

It was my custom to sit on the fire escape in the sweltering evenings and talk to Richard on the phone. It was in this way that I learned about him. I learned that he was working on a full-length film, a project that he and Alex had started in high school together.

"Why don't the two of you talk anymore?" I asked.

He sighed, "He's found better company, I guess."

"Jason? You call that better company? He's as smart as a pile of wood."

"He's popular, rich, well-connected."

I was coming to understand that when Richard said rich he meant really rich. Sure enough, he mentioned on another day that Jason's dad was some big-wig at Google and a Simon College trustee.

"Alex keeps asking me about you. Asking why I'm talking to you..." Why? I bet he did not ask "why" about white girls.

Richard was working at a local diner for the summer and editing film by night. His dad was threatening to cut him off if he didn't start doing pre-law courses and they fought about it at least once a week. Once Richard said that he should have died instead. We were quiet after that, and a minute later, he grumbled that he didn't mean it and I understood.

We followed *American Idol* together and debated over our

favorite singers. We laughed together until I heard the turn of Aunty Sylvia's key in the door every night.

One night, Aunty Sylvia came home with company; two of her grown children. Aunty Sylvia's husband had died a couple of years ago. She never mentioned him, he only watched over the house with a grim and serious face in photographs placed among trinkets around the house. Caribbean men don't smile in photographs.

Cousin Charlie looked like a jollier version of his father – his belly was round and he liked to joke and laugh.

"Mummy, you make me a set ah roti to take? I as be missing your food, you know!"

Aunty Sylvia's lips parted into an awkward smile. So he was the key to her. The woman next to her was called Cousin Joan, a generously proportioned brown-skin woman with her short, relaxed hair combed back into a tiny no-nonsense ponytail. Aunty Sylvia bossed Joan around.

"Joan, I have the chicken in the fridge there, season already. Put it on di fire, nah?" Aunty Sylvia ordered. Joan went and did as she was told. It did not matter that she looked to be in her mid-thirties. This was the way that we understood the world to work.

Aunty Sylvia and Cousin Charlie sat down in the living room and watched Jeopardy and I dared to sit with them. I liked the show. I got too enthusiastic for Aunty Slyvia's taste most nights, yelling out the answers until she complained. "You mus be quiet, gyal. You raisin up me blood pressure!"

On this night, Aunty Slyvia only let me sweep one category before dismissing me from the room.

"Go an help yah cousin in the kitchen."

There was a note of unquestionable finality in everything that Aunty Slyvia said that reminded me of my mother. Knowing that it would be more trouble than it was worth arguing with her, I went and asked Cousin Joan what I could do to help her.

"You know to clap Roti?"

I nodded. Perfectly circular sheets of dough rose and bubble on a black cast iron skillet. I picked the hot roti up quickly, throwing it into the air and clapping the air bubbles flat between my palms.

Joan's thoughts seemed to be lost in the strong smelling green curry. She she spoke suddenly.

"So you're Paul's daughter?" I nodded.

"When was the last time you saw him?"

"I must have been four or five... I don't remember properly." I confessed.

"You?" I asked, expecting to hear that she too had not heard from him in fifteen years.

"I went an see him last year."

"Last year?"

"Come now! Pick up di ting!"

The roti was brown on one side and light on the other. "So, he's not..."

"Dead? Don't be stupid, he livin down by New Amsterdam, deh. Is who tell you he dead?

Yuh mother?"

No, my mother had never said that, but fifteen years of silence had. I couldn't imagine having children and being so willing to abandon them for so many years. I thought back on the lie that I told Richard and the memory twisted like a knife in my stomach.

I was quiet then. I had so many questions that burst and broke like bubbles when I tried to speak them.

"No one ever told you anything about him?" There was a new note of softness in Joan's voice. I shook my head no, sure that she would not consider my mother to be a veritable source.

"Paul is sick now. Sick, sick. But if you livin that way... You can't hide from God." She looked for recognition in my eyes, but I did not understand. Cousin Charlie was howling over some question or answer in the living room.

"He is not a man of God." said Joan flatly. But truthfully, I had known few men of God in my lifetime, and I didn't see why my father should be judged any differently.

"He wanted mummy to take him in, you know. He wanted to come here to America for better medical care, but she ain wan to get mix up in that again." "Mix up in what?" I asked finally.

Joan's brow furrowed. She was angry with me now. I was asking her to say something that she did not want to say.

"Your father is an anti-man. You know what dat is?" I did not answer.

Joan put her focus deep into the steaming curry again.

12

Caityln, Margo, and two older people who I immediately recognized as Caitlyn's parents waited for me at the bus station. Her father had feathery white hair and small, clear blue eyes that felt as if they could look through me. Her mother was a short, thin woman with a thick mane of brownish-auburn hair exactly like Caityn's. The two looked very much alike except her mother always seemed to be smiling as if in anticipation of some future happiness. The mother had laugh lines, while Caitlyn's pale face was cruel and smooth.

"Finally!" Caitlyn complained. "The bus was supposed to arrive, like, fifteen minutes ago." She grabbed my rolling suitcase and headed towards the parking lot. Caitlyn's parents came forward smiling at me and offering their hands for introductions. Caitlyn's father stepped up first.

"Call me Barry." I shook his hand, knowing that I would be calling him Mr. Farley.

"Suzy!" Caitlyn's mother tossed back her thin, white shawl and offered her slender hand.

"We're so excited to meet Caitlyn's friends from school!" She said sweetly.

The two hurried forward as Caitlyn screeched for them to unlock the huge, shiny green Range Rover. Margo put her arm around my shoulder and smiled, the faint freckles on her cheeks had darkened with the summer months.

"So happy you're here. You have no idea!"

The beach house was at the end of a weathered road that turned to dirt and high grass. The house was pristine white and baby blue with charming wooden shutters and a wrap-around porch with a swing. In a lot of ways, it reminded me of the old colonial houses in Georgetown without the flamboyant colors.

A boy with a swoop of hair over his left eye and several earrings adorning his right ear stood waiting for us on the porch, Caitlyn's brother, Caleb.

"Take this." Caitlyn gestured towards my bag. Caleb ignored her and nodded my way.

"Come on, Celestine." Caitlyn scowled. "What a weirdo." she muttered.

The house was much bigger on the inside with a sprawling open plan that seemed to encourage ease and relaxation. The walls were littered with pictures of the perfect family. Pictures in which Caleb's piercings did not make an appearance and Caitlyn seemed younger and happier, grinning toothily despite her multi-colored braces.

Upstairs, Caitlyn got me settled in her room. An extra bed had been pushed into the room which I was told I would share with Gerty.

"Where is Gerty, anyway?" I asked.

"You know Gerty. She's on her own schedule. Says she'll be here in time for dinner."

Caitlyn sank down onto her own bed. The room was mostly bare and the frilly magenta sheets on her bed indicated that she had been sleeping in that bed every summer since before she traded hearts and lace for preppy plaid.

"Have you been here all summer?"

"Only for the last week. Daddy was on business trips most of the summer. He went to Dubai!" she added as if she had been there herself.

"How has your summer been?" Caitlyn regarded me suspiciously as if I could not possibly care.

"It's been a summer. I was busy at my internship mostly." Caitlyn had worked at a fashion magazine throughout the summer, but the details of this internship did not interest me in the least. Caitlyn was usually close-lipped about anything personal. The only exceptions happened when she was drunk. Once, we sat in the stairwell of a senior dorm while a party raged in the basement below. Gerty had run to some room on the top floor where she had apparently left her phone and the two of us waited for her. Caitlyn laid her head in my lap, the glittery eye-shadow that she had applied so diligently two hours before smeared on my black, pencil skirt as she sobbed and burped tequila.

"I think I loved him..." She kept trailing off. After the fourth time she cried the words, I asked her "Who? Caitlyn, who did you love?"

She looked up at me curiously, with that mingled look of disgust, recognition, and misunderstanding that she seemed to reserve just for me.

"Aaron."

After a night of drunken confessions, Caitlyn would be the first of us up in the morning, making her way to the dining hall for early Sunday morning breakfast and studying with militant discipline for the rest of the day.

Gerty arrived in the middle of dinner which consisted of Red Snapper, grilled asparagus and mashed potatoes.

"You must eat fish all of the time in the Caribbean, Celestine." said Suzy. Caitlyn's mother was curious about me. She had already asked if I learned to swim in the ocean (no, the coast is protected by a sea wall). Then she innocently asked if I would like some coconut water. Caitlyn growled "Mom…", but I accepted her offer. I hadn't had coconut water since I left. I sometimes woke in the morning with a taste for it on the back of my tongue.

Gerty entered the house, bursting with energy and confidence. Her skin had browned and her curls had been bleached to a lighter shade of honey brown by seawater and sun. Her restless energy sent a ripple through the room. Caleb slipped easily into the quiet world of Facebook on his phone, scrolling past other friends with tattoos and piercings. I wondered if he had any tattoos. I did a brief scan – he was too bulky for his skinny jeans and I spied the pale skin of his lower back. No, he didn't seem like the type for a lower back tattoo. Next, I looked to his arms, middle build, not too skinny, not too muscular, not too fat, unremarkable arms, really except for the wealth of shimmering reddish-blond hair that covered them like a fog. But no tattoos. As if he had felt my eyes on him, he leaned over to show me a cat meme.

Gerty made her rounds. She hugged Mr. Allen so tightly that the man blushed, uncomfortable. She gave Margo a hard kiss on the forehead, leaving a big, pink stain between the curtains of dark hair.

Then she came to me and squealed "Cele!" with her arms outstretched. Although I usually wanted to be angry with her, I could not help but feel that her being there was a huge relief. Margo was perhaps my closest friend, but Gerty was my first in this country, so I smiled and said, "Hey Gerty,"

She wrapped me in her arms.

"Call me Gertrude now."

She went through this every few months. Every few months she would declare herself Gertrude. But maybe she really was someone new this time because she did a thing that Gerty had never done. She took the liberty of tousling my hair, then kissed me on both cheeks.

Back in Caitlyn's room, Gerty dumped a duffle bag full of liquor wrapped in her nightclothes on the bed. We were all anxious to begin the wild weekend, so it was not difficult for Gerty to get us to drink that night. She brought mixers, cups, cookies, and chips. She fixed us all bitter-tasting cranberry vodkas.

Gerty lived for The Event, and she always delivered. She pulled out her laptop and speakers and began playing Katy Perry. We all knew the words, it was played at every campus party last semester, so we all sang along. It felt like old times, only in a new place.

Caleb wandered into the room and Caitlyn allowed it; that was how drunk she must have been. Margo kept calling "Shots! Shots! Shots!" and we had all heeded the call with spiced rum at least three times. Soon we were all up and dancing and singing and cursing. I wondered at Caitlyn's parents not minding so much ruckus and noise. My own mother would be in my room in a flash with a belt.

Margo stood up and said she was going out for a smoke. Caitlyn seized upon the idea and suggested we all head down to the beach. We packed up the alcohol and headed for the sea. The heat was there, steady beneath the cool ocean breeze. We walked through high grass and hopped a fence, climbed over rocks, and settled on a narrow strip of sand. Where the water met the sand, it sucked and reclaimed land for the sea.

"Should we be worried? About the tides?"

"No more worrying about anything!" Gerty declared.

Margo was laying down in the sand, looking up at the moon. I laid down too with my head just touching hers. She smoked her cigarette, asked me if I wanted a drag. I accepted but quickly passed it back to her. I had forgotten how they made my head spin. Looking up at the moon I thought is that my moon? The very same moon that hung low, brushing the countryside?

"I miss Patty." Margo breathed dreamily.

"You really like her."

"I do. She's so funny and beautiful. I could look at her all day. I did look at her all day, every day this summer. All night when we could help it."

"So, the deal is sealed?"

"Oh, is the deal sealed? That sounds nasty!" Margo laughed. She touched my hand.

"You and Richard? How's that going? You guys been keeping in touch?"

"Yes," When I said that some great pressure in my belly was relieved. But in its place came the question that I had been avoiding all summer. *Was I his girlfriend? Was this a relationship?* If it were, I wouldn't have to ask these questions, right?

I would just know. I thought of asking him all summer, but I didn't want to seem desperate. I liked the way that things were. I liked how he called every night, usually around nine after he had finished his shift at a local diner. In case his father decided to cut him off, he wanted to have a savings fund, but there was no way that one summer of dishwashing would pay the exorbitant tuition. I was sure that he knew this too. The work distracted him. Hearing little snippets of exchanges between father and son over the phone made me feel uncomfortable. Richard's voice was cold and disinterested. I could never quite catch his father's words. They sounded like short grunts. Once he had called me later than usual. At 11:30 PM, I picked up the phone in a whisper, and with the phone cradled between my ear and my shoulder, I managed to climb out, quietly, onto the fire escape.

"I'm drunk." Was the first thing he said. Then he told me about how his father had cheated on his mother when she was sick.

"She would have gotten better if it weren't for that." Before the end of the call, he said,

"Let's just forget about all of this, okay? Forget everything I said."

"Why?"

"It's just better forgotten."

Richard was making industrious work of forgetting, editing film until the wee hours of the morning, and scrubbing melted cheese off plates at night. He did not need another thing to think about, but would wanting a relationship with me be such a burden? Who weighs the burdens of loving someone? I lived with the knowledge perched on my spine that my love, my passion, my essence was as black as my skin and that some would weigh me and find me too much or in another instance, wanting. But Richard was not like that.

The cold water jumped up to Caitlyn's ankles and she screamed on pitch with a dolphin.

I wondered how safe it was for her to be this drunk on the beach. Gerty, hearing her call, ran out to her with equally high-pitched screams of delight at the frothing, cold water. They slapped and kicked up the water, wetting each other like children.

Caleb's tiny portable speaker played top 40 hits and, re-clining, he nodded his head along.

"Hey, Caleb!" A rich, deep voice came from behind us.

Margo lifted her head up from the sand so quickly that some of it flung off her hair and into my face. I wiped the sand away hastily and saw a man in swim shorts with cherry brown skin, soft-looking tufts of black hair covered his chest, and a head full of blacker dark, coiling hair that I immedi-ately wanted to sink my fingers into. Caleb got up, dusting the sand off his backside.

"Aaron, hey dude!" The two shook hands and hugged for a long time like brothers. As the last notes of a techno song rang out, I noticed that there were no more shrieking in the water. My first thought was to worry, but then I saw that Caitlyn had come out of the water and was staring at this man, Aaron, with such malicious intent in her eyes that I was sure she was about to explode. Caitlyn could be an angry drunk. Sober, she was merely irritable.

Aaron stood his ground and Caleb stayed by his side.

"What are you doing here?" Caitlyn asked.

"Caleb invited me."

"He's my friend." Caleb interrupted, "I can invite any one of my friends to anything I want."

Caitlyn's hands balled into small, white knots.

"You fucking asshole! This is exactly why I don't spend time with you. You're so fucking selfish! What about family loyalty?"

"Loyalty? How could I ever be loyal to an entitled brat like you?"

"Wait a minute. Everybody, shut up." Aaron held a finger to his lips and for some reason, both parties were quiet at this. "I'll go. I shouldn't have come. Caity, I wish you all the best. There's no need for this."

"There is a need. I have the need!" Caitlyn picked up a red, solo cup and threw it at him.

Although it missed, some of the liquor inside did spill on his leg.

"Just fucking go already!" Caitlyn's voice was breaking, partially from exhaustion and also, I guessed, from her earlier screams into the ocean. When he turned around and started walking away, her knees buckled and Gerty caught her and laid her out on a large, smooth rock. She cried with her mouth open, her moans could probably be heard across the beach, maybe even up to her parent's house although no one ever came out to investigate. Eventually, Gerty calmed her, running her fingers though Caitlyn's hair and saying funny things. Caitlyn threw up over the side of the rock and we all started to head back to the house. Caleb had left with Aaron, so

Margo and I led the pack, Gerty dragged a stumbling, burping, and once more vomiting Caitlyn along with her.

"Wow! Wow!" Margo kept saying, "You can't tell me that you expected that."

"No, I did not. So, this is Aaron, she only told me about him once..." I recalled the memory. "Obviously, it was something very deep."

"But did you expect him to be Black? Caitlyn and her uptight, Republican ass?" Margo threw her head back in laughter and I laughed a little too. Yes, it did seem a contradiction, but that was what also made it so true. The Caitlyn we knew came after him. She had tried "different" and it had hurt and changed her in a nasty way.

Part II

13

When Richard picked me up from the bus station a week before the first day of the new semester, he looked like a different man – slouched over like the summer had not been kind to him with a scruffy brown beard, but at least he had a tan. I was fascinated with an obsession that white people have with tans, being tanned was good but not if that was your actual skin color. Back in Guyana, I had once found a jar of skin-lightening cream in Anika's dresser. It made my gut wrench and made me ask myself if I wanted it, if I needed it. I was darker than Anika, certainly, and she was using it. But I did not like to presume that I had anyone who would be interested in me, dark or light except for Kelvin and he was insufferable enough as it was. I often thought of the way that I almost bleached my skin, hoping that I would be closer to something I would never be.

In the car, he kissed me.

"How was your summer?" he asked.

"It was strange," I confessed.

"Strange?"

I wanted to tell him about the revelation that I had made about my father; about this longing to see him that would not leave me alone, knowing that he was dying and that time was limited. I couldn't tell him that I had investigated an address for him and that I had been making notes in a brand new notebook of ways to save for a flight back home. I wanted to tell him no more Starbucks or overpriced slices in the pizza shop. No more getting pulled into "special occasion" shopping trips with Gerty who considered every holiday, big or small, or school holiday, to be a cause for shopping trips to the giant mall a few towns over. I would have to try to pick up more hours, but how? I also had to keep my GPA at a B+ or higher as a requirement of my scholarship, how many hours should be parsed to studying? Well, all that was not taken up by class and work and sleep. And Student Council, I remembered with a sigh. But instead, I said, "Brooklyn is a strange place."

He laughed. "That's what they say. I've never been there before. Maybe one day I'll come to visit you."

The image of Richard sitting on Aunty Sylvia's plastic-covered sofa was so ridiculous that I laughed out loud. He took his eyes off the empty, stretching road in front of us to look at me searchingly, his green eyes were dull and flat.

"I'm changing my major. I already have the prerequisites. If I wait another semester, it will be too late to start pre-law and graduate on time. I have to do it now."

"So, you give up?"

"I don't have to be a film minor or an International Studies major to remain interested in those things."

"Yes but, think of all of the pre-law people you know. You'll never see the light of day again."

"I won't be able to go to those parties and get wasted with you and the crew if that's what you're thinking about."

There was a sour stillness after that.

"If you don't like it you don't have to come. Although, you

are the life of the party." I thought I knew him so well. This time, it worked. His lips couldn't help but part into a reluctant smile.

"I could say the same thing to you. You're always complaining about Gerty and Caitlyn and yet it seems like you're still taking marching orders from them."

We breezed by towns in the blink of an eye, snatches of local department stores, craft shops, and post offices.

"Marching orders." I simply repeated the phrase to myself, swashing it around in my mouth, getting the taste of it.

"Oh, come on!" Richard cocked his head to one side and began to impersonate Caitlyn's nasally tone, "I know I'm constantly paying you back-handed compliments and gossiping about you, but will you please come to my beach house?"

His impression of Caitlyn was so spot on that I had to laugh. His face turned serious.

"I heard them once... Caitlyn was pretending to talk like you."

I felt that hollow feeling again, felt his statement dinging around in me like a coin in a vending machine. I thought back for a moment on how I used to go to the nightwater and fill myself with all the things that I loved. Where had it gone now? Maybe I was really empty after all.

Richard continued nervously in my silence. Obviously, he had been meaning to tell me his thoughts on this topic all summer.

"And Gerty, too. Why?"

"She was my - ,"

"First friend? C'mon. You deserve better than that. Are you scared?"

I did not consciously think yes or no, but I nodded my head up and down. He put his right hand on top of mine and steering with his left. "Don't be."

I wanted to be disarmed by him, wanted to know that he would only caress and softly kiss the tender skin beneath my armor. I wanted to believe in him. But I was not really his girlfriend and even if I were, I was not sure that it would make any difference. I took a deep breath, filled my whole hollow body with breath, and exhaled long. "That beard has given you confidence." Richard grinned and stroked the patchy thing.

He dropped me off in front of my new dorm where Margo was waiting for me outside sitting on a Batman-themed beanie bag. She and I would be sharing a room this year. Gerty and Caitlyn had chosen a rickety off-campus apartment with Jason and Alex. Although the place was nicknamed "Rat House" because of a giant rat spotting at an Environmental Sciences departmental mixer who knows how many years ago and had since been refurbished as duplex apartments.

It is standard knowledge, apparently, that after the first year of college, social circles shift and people gain new interests. And so this happened with Caitlyn, Gerty, and I. I was relieved to not have to go through any kind of dramatic friendship breakup. The fact that we now lived on opposite sides of campus, I thought, would do the trick.

Margo and I made fair roommates. Her mess did not touch my side of the room and when a battered, multicolored converse sneaker made its way near my neatly made bed, I simply kicked it back over the equator, a line marked by a mysterious stain in the carpeting. She was rarely in the room since she spent so much time in the Miller Theater where her real-life happened. Many nights she only came to grab clothing, preferring to spend nights with Patty. Richard, as I had predicted, was buried with work by the end of the first week. He made a little home for himself in the library a booth in the far corner of the second floor with books stacked like towers at the entrance of a castle on either side. He ate quick peanut butter and jelly sandwiches there and drank innumerable tiny cups of coffee. On the nights that he came to see me in my room, he smelled earthy and smokey like the joint I knew he had finished on his way, thinking to calm his nerves from the caffeine and get to sleep. These nights, he fell asleep quickly – a fragile sleep you could tell, but sleep.

I hardly had time to worry about friends or a boy who knew my secrets and slept in my bed. The first student council meeting was upon me before I had properly settled into my routine which included a schedule that made me crisscross the campus almost all day every day with awkward hour-long breaks in between. During these breaks, I would find a quiet spot to read, usually somewhere near my next destination, whether it was the bookstore, the library, or the lawn behind the theater where I sometimes saw Margo taking a smoke break outside of the ultra-modern white domed building. For my first two weeks back, I buried myself in student council minutes and old issues of the Simon College Gazette. I wanted to get a sense of what had been done before me on the diversity committee, but only a few articles mentioned the committee at all. When I started digging through old records and budgets and votes, I saw that the committee had changed little since its conception. The committee's main function seemed to be its very existence. The diversity committee existed and that was all.

One Tuesday afternoon after my 19th century America class with the mostly deaf Professor Randolf who said my name with slow relish as if I were a lost love of his, I found myself unoccupied for another hour before my next class began. The campus had no shortage of activities to offer for these gaps in time. There were always club meetings taking place, exhibits on display, and readings taking place somewhere on campus, but I found that I enjoyed my time better on my own.

I grabbed a quick lunch, a chicken sandwich on some sour, seeded bread that Gerty swore by for only 6.99 per loaf at the campus grocery. America's plentiful cup runneth over with the good, the bad, and the completely unnecessary. I knew bread. Plait bread, heavy bread, sweet bread shiny with egg yolk and cane sugar. This bread was for people who were too used to the luxuries of flour and yeast. Walking twenty minutes early to my Haitian Revolution class, I discreetly spit the seeds into a napkin. I planned to read on one of the couches in the downstairs lounge of The Hamilton Center, where two of my four classes took place this semester when a pair of long, shiny dark legs fell in step with mine. I did not know how Lucy stayed so beautiful all of the time, she was a fashionista, always delicately decorated with slinky bracelets and multi-layered necklaces. All of her clothing was purposefully simple and chic and she had the grace and slender shape of a dancer. I remembered what I had promised her last semester and my chest tightened.

"Hey Celestine," she said sweetly. Lucy had a new look for the school year. She had taken down last year's braids and now her natural hair coiled upwards towards the dull September sun.

"Hey, how are you?"

She said nothing, only hugged me, and smiled.

"I like your hair."

"Thanks," She said, running her fingers through the springy coils. "Some girl had the

nerve to ask me if I could move in class just now. Said she couldn't see the board.

So I turned around," Lucy continued, smiling wickedly, "I looked that girl right in her eye. I think she expected me to say sorry and just move."

"What did you say?"

"I'm not stupid. I didn't say anything. I just looked at her and then I turned back around and continued to take my notes."

I hadn't been expecting this tidbit of intrigue, but in that moment I felt whatever it is that ties Black women's souls together like silk scarves.

"On your way to Rat House?" she asked innocently.

It was true that Gerty and Caitlyn's residence was coming up on our right. I tried to think whether she would be home, but unlike the last two semesters, we were not close enough to know each other's schedules. A bike that I was sure belonged to Alex was parked outside.

"No."

We passed the shabby old brick building. There must have

been some bitterness in my tone because Lucy's eyes grew more wicked still.

"Done with them, eh?" The contours of her voice and accent were soothing to me, not quite the same lilt, but something akin to the voices back home. I laughed easily.

"That's what happens. It happened to me too. Be careful. Suddenly your secrets will not be secrets anymore. If they ever were."

I was not sure what had happened to Lucy exactly, but I knew that she referred to the story about the ugly, blond frat boy.

"They'll have you thinking there's something less about you, and that you owe the difference. You got tired of behaving?"

"This is not what I imagined about America." The words felt sticky in my throat as if I should not say them. I didn't want to regret anything about the choice that had brought me so far away from anything familiar. I was determined to make this familiar, to shrug this life on no matter how tight the fit.

"This place is unimaginable." she sighed, "I go here." And just as suddenly as Lucy appeared next to me, she was taking long, elegant strides towards the coffee shop on the opposite side of the street.

I knew that Anika would call before she did. Our nearly twenty years of sisterhood meant that I understood her maybe better than she even understood herself. I knew her thought process, which dots she would connect to which, and how quickly. When I saw her new Facebook profile picture in which she sported a flowing blond weave, six-inch spiked platform heels, and a dress that I would not even have worn as a shirt and seemed to be made up of seat-belt-like material, I knew that some dramatic announcement was forthcoming.

The call came in the middle of dinner with Margo, Gerty, and Caitlyn. Margo was wolfing down a dressing-doused salad with a side of onion rings, her eyes trained on the dining hall doors in search of Patty or one of her theater friends or anyone else, really. Gerty was complaining about the essay that she had already been assigned even though it was only the third week of classes and I was staring numbly into the navy-colored twilight that enveloped the campus through the enormous window next to our table. Ever since the incident at Caitlyn's summer house, her attitude had gone from bad to worse. As usual, she took her frustrations out on those closest to her and on her studies. Even now, a large psychology textbook lay open in front of her tray, which held only a plate of bare, limp lettuce. She held a fork in one hand and a highlighter in the other, ignoring us all completely. I preferred her sulky silence to her rude and humorless conversation.

I was happy to be able to excuse myself when my phone began to vibrate. After hearing about my father, I had been of two minds about telling Anika. Sure, he was her father too, but Anika never seemed as interested in him as I was. Always mimicking our mother, she chose to bury him, and whatever hurt barbed his name, deep down inside of her. Perhaps she knew, perhaps they all knew.

"Hello?"

"What's up, Cele?" In spite of myself, I smiled.

"You the one who call me, stuhpid. What is it you want?"

"I see like ya datin a white boy ova dere!" She giggled gleefully. I sighed. Richard was foolish enough to tag me in one of the pictures that we had taken at a film screening the other day. Margo was in the picture as well, but he put his arm around my shoulder just as the camera flashed.

"None of your business."

"Why ya so serious? You see? That's ya problem. You can't take joke." I walked towards the empty hallways near the girls bathroom. It was best to talk to my family where no one could hear. People stared when they heard the way I spoke with my family as if I were an imposter or spy. All along they thought I was one of the good ones, that I knew how to talk, how to act, but then I went and spoke gibberish over the phone. It was unsettling to them.

"He's fine, though. He 'ave a lot of money?"

"What is it?"

"Hold on, hold on! I'm getting to it. Jesus! I can't ask my sister how she doin?" The line crackled over the silence.

"I gettin married!" Her voice rang with joy and pride. "Tony asked me last night."

A few things immediately came to my mind. The first, I was ashamed of myself for thinking; could she be pregnant? Next, I was sure that she was lying. Anika only ever talked about marriage in the context of marrying Chris Brown. No mere mortal would suffice. The boys she hung out with, who bought her drinks, paid her cellphone bill, and bought her Beyonce albums were just for fun. And lastly, who the hell was Tony? This did not bother me as much since I had long ago given up on keeping track of my sister's boyfriends, but the question of Tony's identity seemed like the safest step.

"Have I met Tony?"

"No, but I haven't really met him either."

"What do you mean?"

"We met on Globe Date."

Suddenly I felt so tired that I could have closed my eyes right there in the quiet hallway. Globe Date was a website where ambitious women, (preferably with made-up faces, good hair, and a nice ass) could be connected with various bachelors from other parts of the world although every smart twenty-something woman in the underdeveloped world was trying to snag a man from the U.S or the U.K. (preferably white and rich). A few of the girls in my year engaged in loud whispers about the website, never including me because, well, the because was written all over my worn uniform shirt and knobby knees. Desperate to fill in the silence, Anika continued.

"We've been talking for, me wanna say, tree, four weeks now. He seems like a good man, Cele. And I'll get to come to America too. He livin in Atlanta. You livin close by dere?"

Still unable to think of what to really say, I simply said "No."

My silence was awkward, I knew. I felt the thin, taut, rope of our sisterhood pull and splinter. I finally thought to say, "Congratulations, Anika." But I must not have sounded congratulatory.

"You think you is the only one good enough for America, good enough for di white man? Tony owns a studio. He saw my YouTube videos and he say he can get me a record deal. Says I'm talented." I could hear her smiling over the line.

"America is a big country, you know!" She reminded me, although I was quite sure that she could not even conceive of this place. "You musn't worry about me outshining you, Cele.

You musn't be jealous, eh!" Her laugh was high-pitched over the line.

I knew then that Anika would be no help in finding our father. Her mind was elsewhere, no longer in Guyana. And I knew that once you began to peer beyond, observing the rest of the world with cautious curiosity until one was sure enough to leave, anything that threatened to chain you to the thick undergrowth of that land would become inconsequential. I knew that to ask her to investigate, as I had hoped to do, would probably result in the disruption of her fantasy. In our family that was not really allowed. The only one able to carry on with more stupidness was Joey, who us women folk could only hope to guide and pacify.

That night in bed, I read about meetings and congresses and treaties until my eyes burned and my stack of notecards that I had been jotting down notes on slid onto the floor. As I picked up the cards, my phone began to ring. It was Richard. I had been expecting this call – it came nearly every night around midnight when the library staff went around and bullied overzealous students out before closing. At first, my heart began to race like it had in old times. I nearly dropped my index cards again. But something stopped my answering the phone, held my gaze on the name "Richard" flashing brightly on the screen, and twisted my stomach. I reclined back onto the bed and fell into a quick and merciful slumber.

14

Don's tall and bulky football player build was intimidating, and he had a way of using it to block both on and off of the football field. For example, on my way to the library, he managed to cut my path off by standing square in the middle of the way. I veered left, and one of his giant shoulders was there to meet me.

"Hold up just a minute, Celestine. Uh, we need to talk about something." His voice faltered for a moment, he sounded unsure. I wanted to hear anything that could make the pompous Don Bradford sound so unsure.

"What is it?"

"Let's go inside. It's freezing out here."

I agreed and followed him inside, past the bustle of students heading off to class and the vacant-eyed people smoking and not talking.

"So you really went through with that proposal, huh?" He asked as we settled into two leather chairs in a cherrywood reading room with antique lamps. It was one of my favorite places to study with Richard. Being there with Don made me feel unsettled, I was conscious of my body.

"What did you think I was doing?"

"Did you ever think to ask me to like, read it over before you submitted it?"

"Why would I need to do that? You've been so disinterested the whole time…"

"It's just that, look, I don't know what you wrote in there, but I heard something bout 'woefully underfunded' and 'low priority on the development of marginalized students' Girl, you can't just write things like that and give it to trustees to read."

"Oh."

"Yeah, 'Oh.' They're *pissed*. You're never hearing back about that thing. They told me. Look, you wanted change and all you've gotten us is hate."

"They already hated us, they were just indifferent."

Don sat back in the red leather chair. He looked kingly, staring forward into the portrait of some old white dude who had probably donated to the school handsomely before we were even allowed to attend. His jaw moves mechanically as if he would sooner grind his teeth down than acknowledge the rage.

"I'm just tryna make it by, you know that? Just like you. Your anger is new, I see that. My anger is old. Have you ever been called a nigger? Straight to your face? Hear everybody laughing, so you laugh a little too, still tryna belong?"

"Have you ever been called an ugly darkie by your own mother?" The words escaped my lips before I could think. He turned to look at me, his eyes scanning me over again, sure that he had missed this about me. His muscular frame relaxed. The arrogant snarl that often twisted his lips disappeared and he looked more helpless than ever.

"Just lay low, okay?"

"I can't believe you're asking me to accept this. I'm not

even asking for more than what we're due. Have you seen the other budgets?" I started searching around in my backpack for the records that I had printed from the school's archives up a few days ago. Don waved away the papers.

"I know."

I ran my fingers through my hair and closed my eyes. My head was throbbing. A headache had bloomed just before I opened my eyes that morning. I had begged Margo to turn off the light as she dressed at 6:30 this morning. I hadn't eaten since the cold cereal I gulped down over a statistics textbook that morning.

"I promised the African dance club." I moaned.

"Tell them you can't do it. It didn't work. Something like that."

"We're putting on a show to raise money so that the instructor can keep coming." Don raised a dark, defined eyebrow, his expression somewhere between surprise and embarrassment.

"You really think that's gonna work?"

"Yes," I said with more confidence than I had.

"I'll put 'African Dance' on the flyer. White people love African dance. I think it ignites some kind of colonial fervor." Don stood up and grabbed his bag, laughing and shaking his head.

"Good luck with that."

"Why does it have to be just good luck? Part of me was hoping you would want to help." I locked eyes with him, hoping that he would finally see something in my face that interested him or would melt his heart with sympathy.

"What could I possibly help with?" he asked, pausing in the doorway.

"You could help us find a space, a venue. You're Mr. Popular, aren't you? See if you can get us two hours in an auditorium with a stage fit for dancing. Maybe an off-campus house or downstairs at the arts center."

"Okay." He said nodding. I had been expecting him to put up more of a fight, ask more questions. "I'll see what I can do."

When Friday night rolled around, I struggled with the urge to go out, let loose, and have fun. Staying inside and studying also appealed to me, but the pressure to party, drink, and be merry was palpable. Weekends are when hookups happen, when friendships disintegrate, when eyes first meet across dance floors. Loud, techno music blasted through the hallways mixed in with the latest hip hop chart-toppers as people pre-gamed for parties. The energy was destructive and contagious. It had been easier by sophomore year when I no longer lived with Gerty, who was a twenty-one-year-old white woman Bacchus in her own right, and lived for the weekend so much that she started preparing on Wednesday with a preliminary liquor run.

This Saturday night, I had a special invitation from the girls from the dance group to hang out.

We would all meet in Janelle's room, which I understood to be the official headquarters for Black girls from what Lucy told me.

The more time I spent hanging out with Lucy, the more I felt my loneliness disappear. In our few times eating lunch together, walking to class together, or studying, she had probably learned more about my life than any one person on campus, including Richard.

"We are like things to them. And I know that you know you're not a thing, but that doesn't change the way he looks at you. Richard's a nice guy. He's a nice guy, he doesn't want to treat his things mean, it's not the kind of guy he is, still, that doesn't mean they can't fall in love with you, but you can't truly love a thing, an object, a static image that only serves your own purposes. You have to love every dimension of a person, accept everything, every story." Lucy told me this quietly as we walked towards Jefferson Hall together.

"That seems cynical."

"Girl, wake up. They were lynching people in this country just fifty years ago."

"No one has tried to lynch me here yet." I tried to laugh, but my mouth had gone dry.

Janelle had a spacious single room in the top corner of Jefferson Hall. The room was decorated with fairy lights and pictures of her family and friends, smiling brown faces peeked out from picture frames in every corner of the room. She had a few plaques on display from dance competitions that she had won before she got here. High heels and strappy sandals of every color shape and color-lined her walls. She was picking up a red, bedazzled peep-toe shoe just as Lucy and I came into the room.

"About time!" Janelle gave us the once-over. I pulled on my mini skirt as if this would make me decent.

"I see someone's trying to look good tonight!" Janelle said, smirking.

Lucy chirped, "I love your hair!" Lucy had a gift for redirecting people. Janelle smiled and tilted her head bashfully.

"What can I say? I'm naturally gifted like that."

Janelle's hair embodied what every Black girl thought she would look like after her first relaxer; it was long, full, and shiny, curling into a perfect "C" at her shoulders. Her red and black dress had a deep V that exposed perfect, brown breasts. Her eyelids had been adorned with lashes that gave her a come-hither look. Pamela and Naomi sat side by side on the bed sipping slowly from red solo cups.

"What are we drinking, ladies?" I asked them.

"Strawberry lemonade surprise," said Naomi.

"The surprise is gin. Lots of it." Pamela was choking on her last sip.

Pam stood up and poured Lucy and I drinks from a pitcher kept in the mini-fridge. I noticed Pam's socks printed with cats vomiting rainbows.

"Those are some great socks, Pam." she looked my way and smiled, nearly spilling the punch.

"Thanks!"

Janelle snorted, "I wonder what she hopes to attract in those tonight."

"Not all of us center our existence around men, Janelle." A resounding "Ohhhhh" sounded from everyone in the room.

"Sorry," Pamela said in a small voice.

"It's okay, Pam. Not all of us can procreate with trees. To each her own, I guess." Janelle went back to applying lip-gloss in the mirror.

Shaking her head, Naomi flipped onto her belly and searched through Janelle's music library from her laptop eventually settling on "Hot in Here" by Nelly. I remember first hearing the song back home in Guyana where Joey sang it as if it hadn't been 90 degrees for the past six weeks.

There was a knock at the door and seconds later Marcus appeared, smiling shyly like he had a secret. Janelle rushed to him and hugged him. He held her by the shoulders and took another look at her.

"So you weren't playing when you said we were going all out tonight!"

Janelle struck a pose. "Yes, bitch! You better believe it!"

I took it upon myself to fix Marcus a drink. He was a campus celebrity, vocal, bright, and funny. He was also one of only a few openly gay Black men on campus, which put him under his own kind of blinding spotlight.

He thanked me as he accepted the drink.

"I haven't seen you here before, Celestine. What, are you getting initiated into the crew?" I giggled nervously and sipped my bitter drink.

"Did you bring the cards?" Lucy called to Marcus.

"I need an update. There have been... developments." Everyone ooed except for me.

"What? He blinked at you? He breathed at you?" Pamela reeled back onto Janelle's bed, clutching her stomach with laughter.

"No, he told me where him and his boys are gonna be tonight." That got everyone's attention.

"Where?"

"Who?" I asked, eager to delve into someone else's love life. I had asked Richard what his plans were for the evening. He said that he was studying for an early midterm on Monday, but would maybe try to come out later if he got enough work done.

"You know that house down Dixon road?" Lucy inquired at large.

"Taylor Hall? I heard it was haunted there." Naomi said nervously.

"There ain't no way in hell you're getting my Black ass to go that far into the wilderness." Janelle chimed in, pouring herself a cup of spiked punch.

"One night!" Lucy pleaded.

"I don't know, there's battle of the bands at The Village Eagle." said Janelle.

Pamela laughed.

"You don't give a fuck about battle of the bands. You just want to flirt with Zach. How can you seriously be pursuing someone in a band called Murphy's Blahh. That's like the worst band name ever."

"Yep, his band sucks, but the sooner they lose the sooner we can get back to his room." A chorus of "oooo" rang out across the room and everyone collapsed in drunken giggles. I did not particularly favor either plan, but I was concerned for Lucy, who seemed to have her mindset on exploring some far reach of the campus on her own.

Marcus slid off his book bag and pulled a long deck of cards out of the front pocket. A hush descended in the room and all of the girls got down on the floor and sat in a circle around

Marcus as he shuffled the cards.

"Lucy, you're first." He clasped his hands together, beaming.

The cards were well worn. The back of each card was an intricate, celestial pattern.

Marcus dealt out four cards in a diamond formation. He turned over the first card. "Seven of Swords for Romance" Marcus announced straight-faced. Everyone held their breath.

"Is that good? It can't be good with that many swords, can it?"

Marcus shook his head solemnly. "Yeah, this means there will be a betrayal for you in the love department. Someone's playing you, sis. Or about to. Sorry but watch ya back, okay?"

Lucy blinked once and then laughed. "Whatever you say."

I could tell she did not believe completely in the power of the cards, or at least if she did, she doubted enough to dismiss them. I myself was skeptical. Back in Guyana, people would have immediately called this evil witchcraft, but here card reading seemed to be more like a quirky hobby to keep friends entertained. One bitter gin punch later, the whole matter was forgotten.

We soon arrived at the crowded jungle party. Students spilled out onto the front lawn, drinking and laughing and dancing. Somehow, Lucy had convinced Marcus and I to venture out to the party with her. I immediately had a visceral reaction to seeing a slew of girls dressed in leopard or zebra print bikinis and boys in loincloths despite the chilly early spring night air. Lucy had only gone into detail about the theme of the party as we made our way over to the far end of campus.

"I knew you guys wouldn't come if I told you. It sounds cheesy, I know."

"Oh I'm not worried about cheesy," Marcus interrupted.

"Shit, I love cheese. If you were taking us to some classy wine and cheese faculty party, that would be one thing, but this? The first person who mentions jungle fever is getting slapped." He declared. We laughed.

"I just want to see if Jonathan is there. He told me he'd meet me there."

"We can check it out for a few minutes, I guess." I sighed. The night was beginning to look like more stress than fun but my head was still swimming with gin and I didn't want to be alone.

Before the group got through the door, Marcus recognized a friend and excused himself. He was one of those intangible friends who seemed to be sought after by everyone he encountered and couldn't be relied on to stay by one's side all night.

Inside the party, Lucy and I lined up to receive a cup of beer from a boy with twigs in his hair. I gulped the cup down rather quickly, eager to numb her mind from the ridiculous scene of white people grinding offbeat to rap music in "jungle" attire.

Lucy was looking around for Jonathan, a desperate, panicked look in her eye. I understood. No one wants to be tricked or misled, but the possibility was all too real for Lucy, for me too. I no longer scanned faces to look for Richard in a crowd. I didn't want everyone to see me missing him. That lonely feeling was for me and me alone.

An unfamiliar group of boys settled next to us after getting their own cups of beer.

"Hey Lucy," said the tallest of the bunch, a boy with sandy brown hair who I sometimes saw riding a bicycle too short for his lengthy legs.

"Hey there, George," Lucy said distractedly, her eyes still scanning the crowd. Then George's friend, a shorter guy with dark hair and eyes spoke to us.

"You ladies must feel in your element here tonight. Jungle vibes and all."

My gut churned, but I kept looking blissfully on into the crowd, hoping that the boys would go away. Lucy looked upon the three young men coldly.

"Not at all, actually."

Just then, a pimply young man with unruly black hair interrupted the conversation, Jonathan. Jon had a sorted reputation around campus. He was known as a creep among female students and a douchebag among his male peers. Both parties agreed that he had bad body odor, most likely due to his excessive workout regimen. He wore Under Armor to class and could often be seen chugging protein shakes. I was surprised that Lucy had not yet gotten the memo.

"Good night ladies. You're both looking fine tonight. If you two ever want to have a Ménage à trois let me know. I'm ready." Jonathan laughed sloppily. He was drunk.

"I brought you ladies drinks," He held forward two sloshed over cups of punch and we accepted. Lucy sipped her drink nervously, trying to hold Jonathan's laser eye connection.

"I have to go to the bathroom." I excused myself and made my way across the dance floor. I thought I ought to give my friend some space. I couldn't believe that was who Lucy had come to see.

In the bathroom, girls were painting their lips heavily and singing to the drifts of a Kesha song that went in and out with the opening and closing of the bathroom door. In the last stall, a girl exclaimed, "I dropped my phone in the toilet!" and everyone makes sympathetic sounds. I concentrated on peeing without letting my butt touch the pee-splashed bowl and thought up an escape route. I checked my phone. Still no text from Richard. I felt stupid for even checking, even hoping.

I looked down at the pinkish-red "Jungle Punch" and spat in the cup. I giggled wildly, how unladylike! It was all so ridiculous, me being at this party. It was only a matter of time before someone came in with Black face on and I was determined to leave before that fateful moment. I flushed the drink down the toilet.

On my way out I bumped into a familiar pair of broad, brown shoulders. Don was wearing leopard print shorts and grinding with a red-headed freshman girl. Our eyes connected for a moment, but I kept marching single-mindedly towards the door.

Outside, the chilly night air gave me goosebumps up and down my arms. I hugged myself to keep warm. It might have been the alcohol, or it might have been the blaring siren going off in my ears, behind my eyes, making it so I couldn't see straight, only stumbling forward with *strong* determination to lay in my bed, rest my head on my pillow, and do whatever I could to quiet my mind. I felt like a champion, a heavyweight boxer who could take hit after hit; my vision was just as twisted. I was almost scared, but some voice told me *"Keep standing, keep walking, you need to rest."*

Finally, making it in one piece, I plopped down in bed, and enjoyed the comfort of my own body, wiggling my toes and rolling around in familiar smelling sheets, taking note of each sensation. Thoughts flew in like apparitions, and I fanned them away. SO *WHAT* about Richard and Don, fuck boys in general, actually. I had no time to poke at that wound that asked if I was unlovable. Is that way Richard won't respond to my text? Why can't Don see me as anything other than a problem to solve, not his ease or his escape? Am I disposable? Why was my father, Paul, able to leave so abruptly, without ever looking back?

Somehow every night ended on this question. And every night, I never had a good answer. I watched the moon from my window, letting its gentle rays bathe me. Behind my eyes, rainbows swirl and patterns spin, light bounces around in my mind. I spent another night trying to understand myself and fix the ways I'm broken with a story. A good one, this time. I picture the nightwater tonight like a deep bathtub, the kind my Aunt Zoe has in her bathroom, filled with lavender buds and rich lemon-scented soapy lather. I sink in and dream.

15

❦

Paul thought of his children every day, hoping that one day his princess Anika would come sashaying down the dirt path that led to his shack. He could hear her six-year-old voice singing at night when he could not sleep. So, he never expected to hear from Celestine, who had always been sullen and shy.

Dear Father,

It's been such a long time since I've talked to you. I didn't think that you were with us anymore, but your sister told me that you live in New Amsterdam now and that you are sick.

I won't attempt to catch you up on fifteen years, but I'm studying in America now. It's lonely, maybe that's why I'm writing to you. I hope I'll get to see you when I go home. Write me back.

Celestine

Paul had the neighbor girl read it aloud to him three times. His eyes had gone bleary two years ago. One day he woke up, opened his eyes and the world was a blur. He was already the village outcast. They said the devil had cursed him for living a wicked life. When news of his diagnosis first got out, a group of men arrived at his door in the middle of the night and would have killed him if he hadn't offered his video equipment instead. Then his living was gone. Most days he stared up into the blistering sun and waited to pass on. The neighbor girl, Nicola, would stop by to leave him food or water.

Sometimes he got her to talk, but she never said much. Her mother didn't like her being near him, talking to him or feeding him. Paul was thankful for her little kindnesses, they kept him alive. Every month, a woman from a local clinic came to drop off an assortment of pills. She did not say anything to him. She simply dropped the bag of pills next to his head as he lay on his cot and left. Nicola could not help but speak up when the letter arrived.

"A man like you have a daughter?" The girl raised an eyebrow.

"You have a pen and paper? You can write her back for me?"

"My writing is not so good." The girl lamented. She hurried away. Paul guessed he might have embarrassed her.

He had one other hope – the nurse who came by every month. By his calculations, her next visit was a week away. She was his only chance at writing back to his daughter, and surely as a nurse, she would likely have enough schooling to complete the task. It would not be easy. The woman did not like him. She more than disliked him, she was disgusted by him, repulsed.

She always made sure not to touch him. She did not talk more than what was necessary and even then, her tone was cold. Even so, the prospect of a new mission, no matter how small, sparked a quickening in his weakened body.

Paul spent enough time thinking about the mistakes he had made in life. Somehow everything boiled down to him being a heathen, a degenerate, an outcast. The problem was innate within him. He had been weak, unable to fight an instinct that he knew from its first dawning was different and wrong. He made a valiant fight of it, he sometimes thought to himself when he could not sleep at night. But eventually, he had come to a point in his life when he no longer wanted to believe he lived in a world where he had to hide himself until death. If there was anything such thing as justice if there was any such thing as freedom, he did not want to go on with his life without at least tasting it, no matter the cost.

Paul and Candice had been childhood friends. The two did everything together until his father taught him with leather belt lashings that dolls and jump rope were not for boys. When his uncle presented him with his first camera at age twelve, it seemed he had finally found a hobby safe from judgment and derision. In fact, his camera made him popular. The tougher street boys always wanted their pictures taken, arms crossed, faces screwed up in scowls. The girls wanted beauty shots. People were willing to pay. He slept with the camera by his side and a blade under his pillow just in case any jealous onlooker got a bad idea. It got out that he slept with a blade and that did even more to secure his masculinity. Now Paul was both talented and dangerous. He was inscrutable and above suspicion to most, but Candice always knew in a blissfully ignorant way.

Neglected by her mother and abused by her father, the girl was desperate for love. Any love. She nursed dreams of becoming a singer and a dancer, a pop star universally adored. She had learned early on that love could coexist with pain, so all throughout her teenage years, Paul looked on as men beat and berated her, all for the promise of a little stage time or background singing on a possible hit record. By the time they were seventeen, Paul had graduated to a handheld camcorder, shooting music videos and funerals, and Candice was becoming vacant behind the eyes, almost broken. It was also around this time that schoolmates began to grow suspicious of Paul's sexuality. He had never had sex or a girlfriend and this was enough to label him as a batty boy.

It was embarrassingly easy to get Candice to become his girlfriend. He simply had to care for her without hurting her. He simply had to listen. He simply had to think of her before himself from time to time. He had to let her weep without flinching or turning away. This behavior was innate to his nature and required little of him. In return, Candice became his "girl". It felt good to be normal for a while. There was a kind of freedom to be had with her, the freedom of anonymity. With her he was just another man with no question marks attached; a well-liked man who was skilled and high in demand. Soon he was a father and normalcy gave way to complacency, and his ego again began to squirm and stir and yearn for more.

As if the universe had heard his cry, one day his sister Sylvia, who was living in

Brooklyn gave him a call and said that Caribbean Life, a New York City newspaper for Caribbean immigrants, was looking for a new head photographer. She encouraged him to apply with his portfolio and use her Brooklyn address on his resume. She even offered to let him stay with her for a while while he gained his footing if he got the position. Then he could bring his family to America as well and start a new life.

Paul did just as she said and applied with his best work. When he got the position, Candice agreed to let him use a good portion of their savings for his travel expenses with the understanding that he would make it back to America and send for her and the children. It seemed like a foolproof plan. Stories of one spouse moving to America to establish themselves and then bringing over the rest of the family were common in Guyana. The difficulty was in aligning the opportunities, funds, and circumstances to achieve the move. It seemed they had all three.

Slyvia hadn't seen her brother since he was a child, and evidently, she still thought of him as a child, purchasing his favorite sweets from the Caribbean bakery in her neighborhood in preparation for his arrival. What she got upon his arrival was a grown man who was a stranger.

Paul left the apartment early and came back in the wee hours of the morning. He liked his job and it afforded him a lot of freedom. He took to the streets of New York's Caribbean enclaves, photographing steel pan bands and youth groups, cricket teams, and church choirs. It was like everything he loved about home but faster, sharper and gritty with the character of New York City. He had always been a social man, but now he was making more friends than he knew what to do with.

People called out his name as he walked the gum-speckled streets. Dice players on street corners paused their games to give him dap. He dropped a quarter in the cup of the homeless man who held the door of the local café every morning, smiling as he was called "A fine young man", and got a free dollar coffee from the waitress inside, Louise, who was a recent immigrant from St.Vincent.

One day the paper assigned him an intern, Hernan, and as Paul shook Hernan's hand for the first time, he felt a drop in his stomach which he mistook for love but was, in fact, an omen that marked the beginning of the end of his time in America. Hernan was a black and Dominican with dark lush curls and deep-set and crafty eyes. The two got along instantly. Hernan had been in the country for 10 years now. He had come over as a teen and he knew the city intimately.

After the two covered Caribbean Fashion Week and a fundraiser for an earthquake in Jamaica, Hernan suggested the two grab a drink together. Hernan's MetroCard had run out and he hopped over the subway turnstile of the A train station, asking Paul if he had ever been to the Lower East Side of Manhattan. Since it was not a Caribbean community, he had never had a reason to go.

Hernan regarded him, crooked his head ever so slightly, and smiled.

"I know some places there you will like, I think."

The two started out at a bar with ridiculously cheap drinks. Sitting in the semi-darkness of the bar, they took shot after shot, trading stories of growing up in their home countries.

"I always felt different from the other boys. For a long time, I did not know why. I didn't know there was anyone else like me."

"What do you mean "like you"?" Paul looked down at his hands, his naked hands. He refused to articulate the reason why he never wore his ring anymore. Hernan sighed, exasperated.

"Typical macho Caribbean man. You're gonna make me spell it out. Let's just say, I never had a crush on any of the *girls* in my class." Hernan laughed.

Paul stood up so quickly that he nearly fell over, forgetting how much he'd had to drink. Hernan grabbed him by the arm, stabilizing him. Paul attempted to shake free from his grip, but Hernan was stronger than he looked.

"I'm just trying to help you. No need to act like an ass."

"I... I'm not like you. I have a wife back home in Guyana." Hernan narrowed his eyes skeptically.

"You are afraid. Best you take another shot."

For a moment, Paul stood, nailed to the spot, the room spinning, lights from a disco ball flashing, music pulsating too loudly in his ears. Eventually, he sat down again and took another shot.

Outside, Hernan and Paul walked with arms draped over each other's shoulders, swerving dangerously down the crowded streets. Hernan stopped, propping Paul up against a phone booth to pull out a cigarette. He offered one to Paul and he accepted.

The next few weeks blurred together in Paul's mind, perhaps because he did not care to remember the details of how quickly he became intoxicated by Hernan and the side of life he revealed. On the flip side of every new pleasure there was fear, the fear of being discovered by his sister, the fear of the drugs Hernan seemed to access so easily, the fear of Hernan's tios and primos, tattooed and pierced men who lingered outside of the apartment building where Hernan lived, engaged in "business". One day, Hernan asked Paul to hold a package for him at his sister's place. It was brick-shaped and wrapped in brown paper and crisscrossed with duct tape inside of a gray plastic bag. Paul did not need to ask questions to know it was illegal. The next day, Hernan did not show for work, and the night after that, the cops came banging on Sylvia's door. When Paul looked out of the peephole he saw blue uniforms lining the dingy walls and dogs big enough to be wolves looking as focused and prepared as their handlers.

And that was it. The American dream had started off beautifully, and just as quickly spiraled out of control. His sister never spoke to him again, but somehow the story of Hernan and their relationship followed him on the plane back home to Guyana. When Paul first came home, he played off the deportation, shrugging off the embarrassment and telling everyone that he had gotten into a tangle with the police. He'd nearly been shot dead, he exaggerated. They were looking for a Black man, height five feet eight inches in a black sweatshirt, which just so happened to be the color he was wearing that day. They'd cornered him in a seedy New York City alley, or on an abandoned basketball court, or even once on an empty subway car. That's when he pulled out his knife –for he always kept his knife on him– and the coppers pulled out their guns. Then they shot and missed, or they shot and he ran, or there was a standoff, and he told these anonymous coppers about how he was an immigrant and didn't know a thing about a crime.

Candice would stand in the living room doorway, her toes wiggling in her house slippers, watching him laugh with friends and reminisce wrongly over a bottle of rum. She was waiting for him to slip or maybe that was how Paul felt. She didn't want to sleep next to him anymore. She didn't look him in the eye when they spoke.

After his HIV diagnosis, the truth didn't even matter. He was kicked out and shunned.

Paul played his story out like a dealer deals cards, a different set of scenes every night. He wondered how he could shuffle the cards to gain some sympathy from the nurse, and reflecting on his pitiful life, decided that he should not speak about his own story at all, but of Celestine, his daughter who he knew so little of in reality, but according to her letter had become just the kind of adult he thought she would be.

Bright and early, Paul heard the hurried steps of the nurse fighting her way through the overgrown grass path that led to his shack and pushing open the creaking wooden door.

"Medic," she said weakly. This was his chance.

"Nurse! Nurse! I just need a moment of your time."

"What yuh want?"

Paul could not see, but he could hear the woman's hand on her hip and her exasperated gaze.

"It's not me, it's my daughter."

"You 'ave a daughter? I pity her."

"I know, I have been a terrible father to her, but she wrote me a letter and I can't see to write her back."

"That's too bad. You shoulda live a better life."

Paul felt the baggie of pills drop on the bed.

"We nah have enough of the medication to go around this week, but I bright yuh what I can. It will have to do."

"You're right, nurse. I lived a wicked life, but my daughter never knew me well enough to be ashamed."

Paul held up the letter, his arm shaking. The paper quivered, suspended in the air. Paul imagined the nurse staring at the page skeptically. Then he felt it get tugged from between his fingertips. There was quiet. She was reading it.

"What a foolish girl. She write pretty, though. Studying in

America? I would say yuh should be proud if I thought yuh had anything to do with raising her." More quiet. She was still examining the letter.

"My little one always talk about going abroad to study. Her little cousins dem laugh, but I

tell her it is possible."

Paul can hear the nurse smiling, even if it has not yet reached her lips, a part of her soul is smiling.

"Can you write her back for me? Please? I don't have much to say. I just wanna say something before I go."

Again, a wavering silence.

"I..I...can't do that, sir. That's not in my job description. I'm just here to drop the medication off an go."

"Please! Not for me. My life is gone and wasted, but if I can do one thing to show her that her father loves her, it might heal some of what I broke. Please. Only a few lines." The nurse kissed her teeth. Paul heard the sound of the paper ripping and thought, by some turn of cruelty, the nurse had decided to destroy the letter.

"Please don't rip it!" he cried out.

"Eh eh! Relax! Yuh have any other paper for me to write on? I will write back on the bottom of this same page."

The letter read:

Dear Celestine,

It is so good to hear from you. I'm sorry that this is our first time exchanging words in so many years. By the letter you sent, I can tell you are a smart, ambitious girl who will go far in life. Although I feel I have no right to say so, I love you.

Your father

16

I remember at age forty-five, Aunt Zoe was still as young and fresh looking as her nieces who sat beside her. It was nice to have a birthday celebration with family for once. Usually, Marvin took her to fancy hotel restaurants with poorly cooked European dishes, but this year, she had convinced him to let them stay home and have a big family dinner. She wanted to spend the day with me. I would be leaving for school in America soon and Aunt Zoe found that she was dreading my departure.

My mother fidgeted in a too-tight red dress at the other end of the table. Zoe followed her sister's eyes to the water-color painting of a house on stilts in blue sea that Marvin's friend from Barbados had gifted him the other day. Candice scowled at the painting, the line in her forehead deepening. When she saw her sister watching her she rolled her eyes. Grandmama Mary could barely be seen behind her elaborate black and white hat, with a purple plume that threatened to take out Anika's eye. Anika was not a patient girl, and had already swatted the feather away once.

"Mama Mary, let me take that hat for you. Church finish since 3 o'clock."

Mama Mary fixed her clouded eyes on Zoe, her bottom lip twitching menacingly. Without waiting for an answer, Zoe swept over to her mother-in-law and plucked the hat from her balding head, leaving wisps of gray-white fuzz suspended above.

"Is Jay coming?" Zoe asked as she went to hang the hat in the foyer.

"Jay? Who is that?" Candice asked.

Every word sounded like an accusation.

"Joey," I translated.

"The other day he tell me 'It's Jay, Auntie'." Zoe impersonated the bored, melancholy tone that her nephew often used when communicating with people over thirty.

"He wants to be like Jay-Z," Anika couldn't help herself. She hated family gatherings the most but making fun of people always brought her out of her shell. "He's ugly enough."

All except for Mama Mary, who was mostly deaf, laughed. The merriment quickly died down when Uncle Marvin entered the dining room. He staggered across the room and sat down at the head of the table. Groaning, he reached for the bottle of rum at the center of the table and poured himself a full glass.

Everyone around the table was quiet and still. Anika was looking down at her nails while Candice and Zoe stared at him expectantly. His eyes were bulging and his skin was shiny with sweat and tears.

"They kill him, kill him in the house with the children and wife watchin." He let out a low pitiful moan. Aunt Zoe was the first to break out of the shock. She rushed to him, tilting his head upwards to meet her face, to look into his eyes.

"Who?"

"Sammie."

Uncle Sammie to me. His name reminded me of uncle

Sam, the American white man with a patriotic suit on. Perhaps Uncle Sammie had been the Guyanese version of Uncle Sam. He owned the people who owned anything in this country. More than a few had lost their lives to him, or so it was rumored. It did not surprise me that such a violent man would meet a violent end.

Uncle Sammie had gotten Uncle Marvin into politics, seated him on councils, made his nephew a career. And now that he was gone, we all knew who was next. My mother slammed her hand down on the table.

"What set ah bullshit is this you all get into?" She locked her eyes on his. "Greed. Nobody give a damn about the country, everyone wants to know what I can I keep in me pocket?

What can I tief? Who can I fool? But not you right, big man?" "Be quiet now, Candice." hissed Aunt Zoe.

"He's just as bad as dem. He like to pretend that he's a saint, and he's the only one who is good, he and his people, but they spend so much time fighting that people are dying." Aunt Zoe slapped her in the face.

Anika gasped. I sprang up to hold Aunt Zoe back. But she did not intend to hit her sister again. Once was enough. Before Zoe turned to walk away, Candice spat on her sister's cream blouse. My stomach churned watching the whitish spit set in and drip down. My appetite was gone.

I looked up to see Joey standing in the doorway, giving us a curious look. I couldn't speak. I couldn't think of what to say to him to explain this and nobody else seemed to even notice he was there. He did a little salute to me and then walked back out the door. Classic Joey, appearing and disappearing like an apparition during times of upheaval.

It came as no surprise to me that Uncle Marvin was dead. We had all expected it ever since that night. But now that her husband was gone, Aunt Zoe was not coping so well. Candice had apparently moved in with her full-time. Aunt Zoe did not get out of bed. Aunt Zoe was never hungry. She had taken time off from the library to mourn, but it was coming up on a year now and she still did not bathe herself regularly.

"What's wrong with her?" I asked my mother over the phone during one of our weekly Friday night chats.

I was walking along the abandoned pathways that crisscrossed the campus alone. Passing by the Simon College sign that stood atop a hill just at the road's bend, welcoming visitors to campus, I started down a stretch of highway, long and skinny like electrical tape, stretching on forever against the dense, green countryside, admiring overgrown barns and tall silos in the distance. Being so far away from any human ear, it was the perfect time to call home.

"I don't know. She sad."

"You mean depressed."

"Don't go and call it all of that. Her husband just died."

"He didn't *just* die, it's been a year now. What you're describing... that's not normal."

"Sometimes I feel scared for her. I want to ask for help. I wish I knew somebody to ask for help. I could go to the conjure woman, Bijou."

"Mummy, no. That woman doesn't have a lick of sense. She's a fraud."

"Okay, okay. I know you're right. But who?"

"She needs a therapist."

"What kinda ting you talking, girl? You stay with those white people for too long."

I was quiet. It felt like she knew that I had been considering therapy. My husband might not have just died but I couldn't help but feel so lost here. It was hard to tell who was friend, who was foe, what was love, what was sex, what constituted progress, which incidents represented setbacks. Sometimes, it all felt like a movie, a daze.

"Go to Mr. Bashir," I said suddenly. I don't know why I hadn't thought of this before.

Mr. Bashir prided himself on being a modern man of science. He had even taught a psychology course or two during his adjunct days. I remember many afternoons pouring over his old textbooks with rapt interest. He would understand.

There were many times in my life when I felt proud of my Uncle Marvin's ambition and position, but more occasions when I wondered whether power was worth the repercussions. Lofty ideals make for sweet dreams and a sense of self-importance, but what about the damage to people who uphold the cause? What about the wife left behind after someone decided his ideas were too dangerous? I thought of my own small position on the diversity committee. It felt good to be advocating for something I believed in and I knew my uncle Marvin would be proud that I was finally using my voice, but with every passing day, the burden grew heavier. The stares, the gossip, the people who had never even spoken to me but felt at ease muttering obscenities at me as I passed them in the hallway. I had upset the delicate balance of power, not only with the dance team and student council but also with Richard. I was not supposed to be heard or desired. I was supposed to be quiet and grateful to be here. I was never supposed to express my full humanity.

After I hung up the phone, I decided to head back to campus as nightfall crept in. But for now, it was all pastures and yellow-green grass on either side as far as the eye could see. The road went uphill, so I enjoyed the illusion that it would soon break off, that I could walk right past the edge and fall. Panting and damp under my arms, I reached the hilltop. Before I could soak in this moment of victory, I saw a large, red Ford pickup truck speeding up the hill. I leaped out of the way, nearly losing my balance. A head popped out of one of the pickup truck windows. A white guy with a backward baseball cap yelled, "Hey, Black chick!" and ducked back into the car.

Walking back, I couldn't make up my mind about the incident. I wasn't offended at all by what the guy had said. I *am* a Black chick. I was more curious about whether they were really trying to run me over, or were they just driving drunk to rap music and saying the "N" word when one appeared before them?

17

That fall semester, I saw less and less of Richard. Texts went unanswered, and we did not seem to bump into each other coincidentally as often as we used to. At first, I reasoned that he was trying to catch up with the other pre-law students. Richard was probably studying furiously, I thought and did not have as much time to go on aimless walks or make silly films with me as the star. It seemed plausible. Until I began to notice his new friends, or rather that he was growing closer to an old friend, Alex, again. Richard sat with Alex and his frat brothers at meals, and from a distance, I watched as the boys laughed and fooled around with each other. He was one of the boys. He fit in seamlessly.

When we crossed paths on campus, Richard averted his eyes and walked by briskly. If I plucked up the courage to stop him, perhaps to tell him about my latest student council woes or invite him to hang out or study, there was a new, prickly stiffness to his demeanor.

"Richard, I just want a minute," I called one morning as I caught up with him leaving the coffee shop with his usual overly sweet and creamy order.

"Celestine, I can't talk right now. I'm late... for something."

"Just hold on. It will only be a minute. I feel like we haven't talked in ages."

I looked him in the eye and could not quite recognize him.

He seemed to be swallowing a part of himself down, making his mouth into a hard line, and his stare distant and cold. It gave me an eerie feeling, like when one knocks at the door to a house and the door swings open, but no one is home.

"Yeah, well, I've been busy."

"But what about - ."

"Listen, we can't... I don't want to talk about you and me anymore, okay?"

"Okay..." I said slowly, my throat feeling dry. "But I thought we were friends?"

For a moment, I thought I saw him. He was scared, confused, unsure, but at least himself again. Then he blinked and was gone.

"Listen, I'm working on my pre-law stuff and I don't have time for... for this anymore." I knew that by *this* he meant me.

"With your frat friends, right?" I said. It was difficult to disguise the note of anger in my voice. Richard turned his back on me. He muttered one more "I have to go" and walked off in the opposite direction.

In my room, I replayed the scene again and again in my head. I allowed myself to cry silently for a few minutes. It was not that this conversation had been unexpected. I had felt it in looks and absence of looks, and heard it in the roaring silence between us for some time now.

But still, the confirmation hurt.

Lucy came over with two cups of hot Chamomile tea and I confided in her as we sipped gingerly. She whistled.

"Well, I hate to say I told you so. White boys gonna white. That's the risk you take. They'll pick you up and put you down just like that." she snapped her fingers.

I knew Lucy was right but wished she wasn't so callous about it. A wicked smile parted her plump lips.

"You are still his toy though. Think about it. If you want to get his attention, why not play with someone else?"

"You're awful." I moaned into my tea.

"No, he's awful. Get it right."

"How do you know all of this?" I sat up in the bed too quickly and my head started spinning. I was still light-headed from crying.

"Four years of boarding school in London plus two years of this bullshit. This is the eternal Black girl white spaces dilemma. Black guys are too busy fucking white girls. They see you, but right now you are their *'sistah'* " She laughed at this. "The white boys think you are exotic, an adventure. Kind of like when white people go poaching rhinos and lions in Africa. You represent a thrill. Then you get to hang on the wall of a study somewhere, lucky you."

Lucy grabbed her backpack and pulled out a flyer for the dance concert, splaying it across the bed with pride.

"Listen, cry about him for a few days, but not too long, okay? Then you have to focus on this," she said, pointing to the flyer. "*This* needs you more. Channel your anger into making this show spectacular. The best revenge is your survival."

I nodded stiffly. For a moment I had forgotten myself and what really mattered. The work. Love had never been in the cards for me. I thought I had felt it for a moment, but it was actually a cruel, elaborate distraction. My judgment had been clouded, but now I felt I could finally see again. And I was angry, but my vision had never been more clear.

18

Barack Obama. The name felt clumsy and foreign on the tongue. Not English like the Ralphs, Richards, and George's in my primary school classes; Black boys given fine English names as a matter of survival. Barack Obama was decidedly someone else.

It had not occurred to me that the cookie-cutter American life I sought when I was in Guyana had already been disrupted by this man, this anomaly, Barack Obama. I had heard the name before. Uncle Marvin adored the man and had been tracking his political career for some time now. When I dared to visit my uncle's office at the back of the house he shared with Aunt Zoe in Georgetown, I admired a small section of wall near his desk dedicated to magazine clippings of Obama. Young, I thought, handsome and carrying a demeanor of unshakable confidence that alternately made me believe in him or think him a very foolhardy upstart.

His words embodied optimism so pure they produced a heady sensation, like sugar at the bottom of a coffee cup. He painted America to be the place we all wanted to believe it was. He made freedom, equality, and decent living seem like the natural order of things, hidden only thinly beneath stagnation and cynicism. This Black man was offering America a chance to be good again, if not for the first time in the country's history.

Uncle Marvin certainly thought of him as an idol. Aunt Zoe once said that Obama had inspired him to enter Guyanese politics and bridge the racial and social divides in our country.

Like Obama, Uncle Marvin took up healthcare as his number one cause, something that was sorely needed in Guyana where healthcare was scarce at its worst and sketchy at its best.

Halfway across the world, Obama's message of hope rippled into everyday lives and high-level politics.

Uncle Marvin's death felt like the first shoe to drop. It felt as if it shouldn't have been so, but it was, and that meant that anything else, any other bright and shining banner, could be torn down with just as much momentum, fervor, and ease.

Still, I entered Simon College on the cusp of an election year, and whatever ugliness lay beneath the surface, the students, for the most part, called themselves liberal. Beyond liberal or conservative, they were young and hopeful people, utterly taken by the charm, grace, wit, and sensitivity of Barack Obama. The Black girls were in love with his wife, Michelle.

One October afternoon, Lucy and I lay on the lawn behind her dorm as she scrolled through pictures of Michelle on the campaign trail on her phone.

"Look at her. She's giving us a face. She's giving us hair. She's giving us arms. I want arm muscles now, by the way. My arms are way too skinny." she made a fist and curled her arm.

Sure enough, only two small beans rose from her cocoa skin.

Naomi exited through the back of the dorm and made her

way towards us. She was friendlier with me now that she had seen me hanging with the dancers more often.

"What are you two doing?" she plopped herself down next to Lucy's pile of library books and picked each one up casually for examination.

"Look at Michelle!" Lucy shoved her phone in front of Naomi's face, knowing the picture would not disappoint.

"She's fabulous." Naomi agreed, "They're in Michigan now. I heard rumors that she's coming here to give a speech."

"Shut up!" Lucy cried, a little too aggressively.

"No, it's true… or at least it's true like I said, I've heard rumors."

"Don't let me find out you're lying to me, Nay-nay."

Naomi grimaced at the nickname. It was an inside joke, something they would never say around the white majority, lest they believe "ghetto" was all they were.

Obama "Hope" signs appeared around campus. Students were organizing to go campaigning. Margo had signed up and purchased an indecent amount of Obama/Biden apparel and memorabilia which now littered the dorm room. One night, returning from the library, I tripped painfully on an Obama Pez dispenser, which I picked up and threw at Margo's sleeping lump of a body.

Although things had chilled between Richard and I since the start of term, I noticed that he was active in the election fervor. He was signing people up to vote, which was of particular importance in the Midwest where the vote could go either way. Of course, the Obamas would win their home state of Illinois, but Indiana was another matter. None of the Black kids much fancied going out into the rural heart of white

America to knock on doors, and so as usual, I admired his willingness to put his neck out for me metaphorically if not in a practical day-to-day sense on campus. On that front, I felt quite abandoned.

Soon it was officially announced that Michelle Obama would indeed be visiting campus.

That morning, I dressed carefully in my best attire; a bright red knee-length dress and a matching beaded necklace tied neatly around the neck, a gift Aunt Zoe had given me from her own jewelry box before my departure. I wanted to be perfect for Michelle.

People arrived at the athletic center in droves. Students and professors joined by voters from surrounding towns crowded the basketball arena. I found myself wading through the crowd towards the stage set up front and center. On the stage, government agents milled about with purpose. The crowd, packed in like sardines, was growing restless. It was evident that the lady of the hour would soon arrive.

Something told me to look up. I caught sight of Richard, who was pacing back and forth in the stands, observing the crowd below, keeping his distance and knowing his place in that moment. He could have been glowing. He could have been the only man in the room the way that he stood out. I felt that he was unquestionably mine in a way I could not explain. I waved to him and he could not help but smile.

When Michelle entered the room, the crowds parted like Moses parting the red sea. She spoke with well-paced grace and intelligence, every moment of her decorated Ivy League education on full display, and she spoke with a heart like no one in the room had ever witnessed before. She spoke of a better future for the world, and for the first time ever, I believed that she meant me too - me the immigrant, me the Black person, me the girl. I was transfixed. It was not until she finished that I realized I was crying. As she made her way through the crowd, I wiped away my tears. Before I knew it, she was in front of me meeting my eye and waving my way. I waved back and it was the single best moment since I stepped onto American soil.

Afterward, the massive crowd poured out of the athletic center. Richard and I somehow fell into stride with each other. We were blabbering at each other excitedly, recounting every moment of the evening.

I could feel people respecting me just a little bit more. I could see it in their eyes and the way I was given space. I felt more like a person and less like a stigma. Michelle's aura had done that for me, if only for a day.

"It feels okay to me be today." I sighed. Richard squeezed my hand gently as if he were happy to be with me just then too.

19

I never thought of taking drugs to study, but apparently, that was a thing to do. Indeed, the whole campus seemed to be buzzing with artificial energy. The straight-laced students only refueled with coffee, but others turned to harder drugs, snorting Adderall in the library bathroom stalls.

Those who crumbled under stress were showing signs of fracture. Signs of wear. Gerty's cheek was pressed against the cool desk as she stared with dead eyes at the flashcards fanned out before her.

"I can't study anymore," she groaned.

A gentle summer breeze blew in the cracked stained glass window of the third-floor reading room that we had claimed for study. Pink white petals from a nearby magnolia tree fluttered by, swirling in the summer breeze. It didn't seem right that we should be so miserable while it was this beautiful outside. We tried studying outside earlier in the week, but people kept passing by and Gerty couldn't resist striking up a conversation.

I had carefully planned my schedule to exclude Gerty next semester and was determined to make this our last finals week studying together. Although she annoyed me, even I had to admit that I was tired.

"I've got a little something-something," said Gerty, reaching for her satchel and pulling out a silver flask.

"You can't be serious."

"Oh, I'm serious. Fuck this test. We've been studying for ages. We know everything there is to know." She took an expert swig and then handed the flask to me.

"What is it?"

"Vodka."

"Oh, God, Gerty."

She shook her curls irritably, "Let's go. Bottom's up!"

For some inexplicable reason, I took a gulp from Gerty's flask. She pulled me up from my chair.

"Let's get out of here. Some peeps are chillin at Rat House. Want to come over?"

"Who are peeps?"

Gerty rolled her eyes and let out an exasperated sigh.

"So Jason, Alex, and company?"

"Oh, Celestine. Don't be a drag. Please, just let go for once. The world isn't going to end if you don't get an A-plus," She spat.

Little did she know that the world might very well end for me if my grades weren't perfect. I would lose my scholarship and be forced to leave school and find a way to stay in the country. Aunty Sylvia would likely do her best for me, but really it would be up to me to carve a new life in this wide expanse of a country. I was too embarrassed to tell her this though, so maybe it really wasn't her fault that she didn't understand.

I also knew that I had learned everything there was to know about Colonialism in India and the British East India Company and that my brain couldn't take another moment of it. With a knot in my stomach and my head floating in tired delirium, I followed her into the lion's den.

The door to Rat House was wide open and I could hear party music blasting from the backyard. I had only expected to see, Jason, Alex, and perhaps Caitlyn, but now I could see that there would be extended family at Rat house this afternoon. The who's who of campus scattered around the living room and pouring into the backyard where a beer pong game raged on.

"Looks like one everyone else is sick of studying too," I admitted, taking stock of the crowd. A healthy sprinkling of frat boys, a few crossover hipsters, and a handful of student-athletes. In the kitchen, Gerty made sloppy drinks.

"Just be cool around Jason, okay?"

"Be cool? What does that mean?"

"I mean don't ask him Student Council stuff. You're obsessed." "I'm not obsessed!" I insisted.

Posters had just gone up for the African Dance Extravaganza, and that seemed to irritate Gerty. Well, not so much Gerty, but Gerty's boo thang, Jason.

Jason says it's disrespectful, going over the heads of the Student Council to raise money.

Okay, so what would Jason recommend, Gerty? That these programs remain underfunded?

Jason says you talk too much.

He doesn't like his women mouthy. You're seriously crushing on this asshole?

I did not know how to be around Jason. At first, I thought it was best to just be silent, but then he would stoke conversation, locking his eyes on mine. Like most men, he couldn't stand to be ignored, regardless of whether he even liked the person or not. In our interactions, I felt that he was asking for something that I could not, would not give; some kind of deference that I did not feel and could not fake. The best solution was to avoid him, but with Gerty around it was impossible. Until I finally said it to her face, told her to leave me alone and that I didn't want to be friends, I had no hope of ending this cycle. She seemed content to keep me, her grumpy little pet.

Gerty pounded down her drink and burped. At the prospect of facing this crowd sober, I tipped my own drink back. My eyes searched around for Jason, perhaps just as intently as Gerty's did. I managed to avoid him two times. Once ducking into the bathroom and next by starting a conversation with a girl that sat near me in sociology class. Somehow, I found myself sitting against the back fence, 4th in a row, receiving a drag on a joint every so often as the sun disappeared and Gerty turned on the fairy lights. I sat with my hands around my knees, thinking that I should go. But I stayed, wondering if Richard would show up. Ever since that night last September, I wanted to relive that innocence. When we only had ideas of each other. Our love was new, malleable, negotiable, mostly just yearning.

Instead of hearing Richard call my name, I heard the nasally tone of Jason Feltman. At first, I ignored him when he called "Celestine" as if there could be another girl here with that name. Then I thought, he might not like that, but it was too late. He was walking over.

"Hey, Celestine."

"Oh, hey," I said weakly.

"You wanna play beer pong?"

"No thanks." Smiling for him always felt painful like my jaw was wired shut.

"Why not? You're not mad at me, right? We're all good?" He laughed nervously, flashing his charming smile.

"Yes, of course!" I said instantly, laughing a hollow laugh. Then I said, "Why wouldn't we be?"

He raised his eyebrows and shrugged his massive shoulders.

"I don't know. I just hope there were no hard feelings, you know, about the funding. Rules are rules, sometimes the law has to come down and - blam! - tell it like it is." I wished that he would stop talking and go away because I was thinking dangerous thoughts.

Thoughts that were "not cool" by Gerty's estimation. I swallowed my spit and nodded.

"I see you're helping to organize the dance thing."

"The African Dance Extravaganza," The act of saying those words aloud lifted a latch in my spirit.

"Yeah, the African dance thing."

"I hope to see you there." I drew myself up to full length, which only hit Jason's bicep, but still, he regarded me with some alarm as if I stood seven feet tall.

"I doubt it."

"Oh yeah? Why not?"

"Not really my crowd."

I didn't say anything. It was past time to go. Apparently, our interaction was gathering attention around the yard, people stared as they danced offbeat. Alex and a few other cronies gathered in with interest. I started walking away.

"Where are you going?" he put a firm hand on my shoulder. "We're just talking. No need to get mad."

"I'm not mad, I'm just leaving."

"So, you're fucking Richard? How is that? He seems like a pretty weird dude to me. Does he make you do any freaky-deeky African shit?" Jason was talking quite loudly. A few people around us gasped, then giggled or whispered. Gerty made her way into the growing circle.

"Jason, stop it. Stop being such a douchebag already. We get it." Red-faced, Jason turned to Gerty.

"Will you shut the fuck up?"

Gerty's face crumpled, and she ran back into the house. Instinctually, I ran after her, shoving Jason aside and running swiftly with my stomach spinning. Behind me, I could hear someone call "ugly slut" loud and clear above the music.

I caught up to Gerty before she could lock her bedroom door.

"Get out!" she wailed. It was jarring to see Gerty in such despair. She was the life of the party, the forever optimist, the queen of corny jokes and yet now she just looked like a girl. Her make-up was smeared, her skirt crooked. She looked broken.

"I'm tired of you." She moaned through her fingers. "I'm tired of all of the bullshit that follows you."

"Imagine living it. But you can't. God forbid if even for a moment you thought about someone else..."

"Think of someone else? What do you call this friendship? I'm doing you a favor. I'm too fucking nice, that's what Jason says."

"The same Jason that just told you to shut the fuck up? I know it's what people say, but

are you really that stupid?"

It was enough. She glared up at me, eyes bloodshot and teary. I knew that our friendship was over and so I left.

I kept playing the scene over and over again in my mind. Gerty crumpled on the floor, completely immobilized in her victimhood, unable to stand, but instead cowering beneath me.

Where was her unbreakable confidence? I had always admired her ability to keep on being herself, wearing tutu skirts to class and passing out in a hungover haze, but waking just in time to dominate the class discussion with conspiracy theories until the professor asked if they could hear from another student.

20

The first light of morning poured in over Margo's Abbey Road poster. It was the first thing I saw every morning. Beneath the poster, Margo and Patty were tangled together, wrapped up in thin cotton sheets and underthings. The pale morning sun christened their bodies too, Margo's honey brown skin and Patty's chubby, freckled arms.

I had never known an openly gay couple in Guyana, where homosexuality is taboo, and I certainly hadn't told my family that my roommate was gay. They had never asked. I imagined my mother would be disgusted, but I felt protective over the couple. There was a bond to be found in being different on this campus. Just existing, let alone existing proudly took a certain amount of gall.

Freshman year, Margo had been miserable and lonely, entertaining a string of subpar hook-ups that had hollowed her out, and left a depressed shell of a person. That all ended when Patty came into her life and made her believe in people again.

I smiled to myself watching the two. Margo tossed and turned, knocking a library book onto the floor near the foot of the bed and shouldering Patty in the face. Patty gave a defiant

shove back. Is this what it had looked like those few early days with Richard? No, I had been curled up at the edge of the bed thinking that I should not feel like a secret. Was not the goal to end up in a man's bed? No, the goal was to be wanted, fully wanted mind, body. and soul. The goal was to belong to him like how Patty and Margo seemed to belong to each other, their bodies flowing together, cradling each other.

Suddenly there was a loud rap at the door. I was still groggy with sleep and called over to Margo to answer the door. Margo was the one with friends, the one with visitors at all times of day and night. Theater people and Rugby players stopped in regularly, looking for one or both of the dynamic couple.

There was another loud knock.

"Margo," I murmured.

"Margarita!" called a voice shrill as a siren from the hallway.

At that, Margo bolted up, her long, black curls flying every which way, her eyes pinned wide open. She stared at the door as if waiting for confirmation.

"Margarita Christina Selano, abre la puerta!"

Two more loud bangs. Patty's head of bright orange hair appeared next to Margo, her eyes still squinty with sleep. Margo mouthed "under the bed," Patty mouthed back "What the fuck?" Margo mouthed, "It's my mom. GET UNDER THE BED!" She gestured with her hands to emphasize the point.

Patty pulled on Margo's David Bowie t-shirt and ducked under the bed in her undies. It was crowded underneath Margo's bed, suitcases, piles of old notebooks, a guitar case, more than a few empty bottles of wine and odd shoes made for an uncomfortable fit.

"Coming!" Margo called in a nervous baby voice as she

pulled on a t-shirt and stumbled to the door. Mrs. Selano nearly ran Margo over as she busted into the room. Her skin was fair, and her hair recently dyed jet black. From beneath heavy eyelashes, she surveyed the room, her eyes resting momentarily on me as I nervously adjusting my silk headscarf. Mrs. Selano smiled at me, "Sorry to wake you, niña."

Margo's eyes were blank with fear. She dared not look down towards Patty, who I could not help but notice was doing a poor job at hiding.

"You're sleeping late, Margarita. You should be up and studying. What about biology? I thought you said you failed biology?"

"I didn't say I failed. I said I might not pass."

Mrs. Selano turned her sharp eyes to her daughter. Margo wilted under her mother's gaze. Mrs. Selano was not very tall, but her six-inch espadrilles made up for it. She wore a pink linen dress and a light, airy Sunday hat with flamboyant flowers and lavender sprigs pluming from the bouquet. No one would expect her and Margo to know each other let alone be mother and daughter.

"I thought you said the Christening was next week? When I'd be home?" asked Margo in a thin voice.

"I never said this, Margarita. Is this what you sleep in? Where is the nightgown I sent you?"

I got a flashback of Margo throwing the lacy, blue nightgown into a clothing donation box for the county homeless shelter, deciding that it would better serve "Some miserable little brat" than she who slept in tee shirts or nude most nights.

Not a hint of snark or sass could be detected from Margo

as she stood now with her fingers linked behind her back like a schoolgirl in the principal's office.

"The Christening is now in 2 hours. Get dressed!" She gave Margo a small slap on the thigh like a racing horse.

"I hope you have something decent to wear," Margo slowly moved towards her wardrobe to pick an outfit. Her mother hovered behind her, doing a quick, critical evaluation of every piece in the closet.

"Why do you dress like a gothic person?"

I got out of bed and gathered my things for the shower. The bathroom was right next to our room and if you went to the final shower stall, and listened at the window, you could hear all the goings-on. It was better to be at a safe distance it seemed. I wanted to give Margo and her mom some privacy, but still, hear all of the highlights.

In the bathroom, I tiptoed around the drain in my shower slippers, avoiding the mass of hair spread over it like an intricate spider web; silver blond hairs, wavy brown hairs. I collected my own kinky hairs for the garbage where stray hair belongs.

Warm water running into my ears, I listened to Margo and her mom go back and forth about outfits when suddenly the water went icy cold. I jumped back, grabbing onto the soap dish for support. From the window, I heard Mrs. Selano call "Margarita!" with fire in her throat.

"Mami!" Margo squealed through a closed throat. She was crying.

"Margarita, why is there a white girl underneath your bed?" "Let me go!" screamed Patty.

I strained to hear more, but a second later the bathroom

door clattered open. I peeked out and tied a towel around my body. Patty was bracing herself on the sink. Her face was red and tears were streaming down her cheeks. She considered herself in the mirror, running her fingers through her fiery red hair.

"What a bitch." her voice was breaking. I noticed a bright red hand and nail marks on

Patty's left bicep.

"What happened?" I asked, adjusting my shower cap, which had fallen over my eyes in my haste. Patty was full-on crying now.

"Her mom's a psycho bitch. I have to go back."

Patty headed back towards the room and I followed. With the door still open, Mrs. Selano was screaming and crying and cursing in Spanish. She teetered over Margo, who was curled up crying on the bed. Mrs. Selano held her left espadrille in her hand and repeatedly hit Margo with the frilly shoe.

"I pray to all the saints to save you. Someone save my baby. Someone save my little girl!" Patty attempted to tackle the woman, but Margo's mom threw her off with ease.

"Get out of here, you nasty dyke!" Mrs. Selano's mascara was running. Patty lay on the floor, propped up by her elbows, tears flowing freely down her ruddy cheeks.

"Stop it! For God's sake, stop it!" I cried. I held the woman's arm gently, but firmly. I had expected that Mrs. Selano would turn on me next, but instead, she buried her face in the fluffy, teal towel that covered my damp chest, sobbing loudly like a widow.

21

The invitation came in the form of an innocuous-looking email.

Subject: Touching Base. Sender: Kiyanna Hall.

I first met Professor Hall during summer orientation. She was the head of the Diversity and Inclusion department and taught the only African American Lit class on offer. Ms. Hall had gently pressed me to take her class as she guided the diverse group of freshmen through the registration process, but I had no interest in poems or novels. My Grandfather had always said "One must know fact before reading fiction." and I tended to agree. Still, after the perceived slight on registration day, Professor Hall became cold towards me and we did not speak again. The message was vague. Professor Hall wanted to "catch up" (on what?) and "check-in" as if we were actually good friends. The last line read like a court date: "I look forward to seeing you in the Bookman building on April 28th at 4:30 PM."

Of course, I knew what the meeting would be about. I brought my carefully curated file on her Diversity Council projects which stretched far beyond student council.

In the past few weeks, stares and whispers followed me around campus. There was even a rumor that I might be "ejected from my seat" which always made me laugh as I instantly imagine myself projected up into the air during a student council meeting, punching through the ceiling with my newfound strength and soaring above the campus, on to elsewhere.

The buzz was good for ticket sales. The show was a little over a week away, and the tickets were already sold out. I had encountered two torn posters and one with a swastika drawn on it in red marker, but luckily, I always carried extra copies. I had even brought a few to hang in the Diversity and Inclusion office.

The entire Bookman building had the feel of a dank and neglected basement. It was home to the student development office, where one could sign up for work-study jobs and attend info sessions for Green Peace. I sat down on the stiff, discolored couch facing three closed office doors. I observed the posters plastered on the ugly yellow brick walls "Top 10 Interview Tips" with happy-looking young people in ties and pants suits, recruitment posters for top graduate programs, a poster calling for volunteers at the local high school, everything a wholesome young person could hope for to become a useful member of society.

Professor Hall peeked out her office door, scanning the waiting area quickly as if she expected to find no one. I waved cheerily, and Professor Hall opened the door wider, revealing her soft shape, 5'6" in linen pants and clogs. Her pale brown face was curtained by limp brownish-gray curls and her green tortoiseshell glasses magnified her tiny eyes.

"Hey Celestine!" she rolled her neck in a "Black girl" way that was embarrassing for both of us.

Professor Hall's office was spacious and neat. I was careful to take stock of every professor's office; they were among my favorite places on campus. There was something about a personal room dedicated to academic pursuits that I found irresistible. I liked the shiny plaques with the professor's name inscribed, I liked the degrees and awards framed on the walls, I liked the mile-high bookshelves and plushy chairs. I sat myself down in one such studded leather chair and allowed myself to sink in. Deep down in my subconscious, I thought I might like to have an office like this one day. I would decorate it with objects that needed explanation; rare maps and artifacts I would warn visitors not to touch in a kind, clipped voice, and a framed photo of Barack and Michelle Obama on the wall. Professor Hall cleared her throat, interrupting my musings.

"So, how have you been?"

It would be one of those meetings where they danced around topics and tried to pull hard words out like scarves from a magician's mouth. I fidgeted in my seat. How could I sum up the last two years since we last spoke?

"Fine. Good, even." I said smiling. I did not intend to make this easy.

"So, you joined the student council. How has that been?"

"Mostly boring," I said earnestly. I had recently begun doing my class readings during the meetings. Last time Jason called me out on it, hoping to humiliate me.

"Oh? It sounds very exciting from what I heard. You wrote a proposal for the Diversity Council's budget to be expanded. You're raising money to bring another dance teacher to campus?"

It occurred to me that Lucy must have approached Professor Hall for help to bring Saffiya to campus. I had been the last resort.

"Yes, I'm trying to do all of what's in my power."

"It's a lot for a sophomore to take on," Professor Hall tapped a document on her desk, the proposal. "This is very impressive. Nicely written."

"Thank you."

"Where are you from again? Forgive me, I forget."

"Guyana, professor. It's an English-speaking country. I learned to write from my grandfather, who was a professor, and my aunt, who is a librarian."

I had this line prepared for professors who questioned where I had learned to write so well. Freshman year, a professor had even accused me of plagiarism. I expected this curiosity from white professors, but I found the inquiry annoying coming from Professor Hall. It reminded me that there is only so much kinship in melanin. To the Black Americans, I was still "other."

"Wow, that's lovely." Professor Hall smiled too wide. I shifted in my seat, hoping the warm leather would consume me.

"Is there a problem we have to discuss?"

Professor Hall raised her feathery eyebrows. I had forgotten to be soft and accommodating, a mistake I often made here. Americans don't like to speak directly. Questions must be punctuated with smiles, commands clouded by "if's" and "maybe" or negated by "sorry."

"It's just, you've chosen to take such a nontraditional route with this issue. Usually, efforts like this take coordination with the administration. There is paperwork and a system of review; a process."

"The process was not working, Professor. I understand that my proposal was rejected. I was told this, although I never received formal notification."

"Right," Professor Hall pressed her fingertips together in thought. "Well, your willingness to proceed with your plan, even though it was officially rejected, has not been... ehm... well received by the administration. Some wonder if it's a sign of a behavioral issue."

"I know how to behave, professor. I raise my hand in class and take notes. I get good marks and follow the campus rules. That's more than I can say about most of the students on this campus."

"That's up for debate," said Professor Hall flatly, "Frankly, this dance show you're putting on - ."

"The African Dance Extravaganza," I interjected. I had taken such care in naming the event. The least others could do was say the name.

"Yes, the dance extravaganza. It's causing quite a stir on campus. I'm afraid for your safety and the dancers' safety. The fact is, people plan to protest and I'm not sure what the nature of the protest will be."

"But what is there to protest? It's a dance show. Unless you are telling me that students plan to protest the color of our skin. If so, why should we get in trouble for it? What about the racist students who hate us so much that they will not allow us to dance or celebrate our ancestry?"

I felt my chest growing tight, my blood pumping hot and acidic. Without thinking, my nails pressed into the leather armchair as I held back the urge to really "misbehave". Professor Hall clicked at her computer, then turned the monitor towards me.

I saw a full-screen image of my student council photo with "BEWARE ANGRY BLACK WOMAN" written in bold, red letters across my features. Beneath there were comments, laughing emojis, bitch, nigger, cunt, illegal, coon, slut. I absorbed the words one by one Before finally turning away.

"This was found in a private chat group and reported by a student. I don't mean to frighten you; I just want you to know that the threat is real. This is a sensitive situation. Anything you do to agitate the situation might cost you your scholarship."

I had no thoughts, I was numb. What professor Hall was telling me went beyond reason. Reason says that good will always win out. Reason says I should not lose my scholarship to hate. I found myself standing.

"So, what does "agitate" mean? Proceed with the show? Am I supposed to cancel?"

Again, Professor Hall pressed her cubby fingers together, her lips pursed, her eyes expressionless.

"You're just the messenger. They used you."

"Now, Celestine, there's no need to -."

"You're meant to keep the brown kids in check. Is that it?"

"That's not fair."

"No, this isn't fair. This!" I fling my arms around, gesturing wildly, to the office, to the campus, to this bizarre country that thrived on a flawed idea of equality. At least in Guyana, no one expected life to be fair.

2 2

Lucy was not at the designated breakfast meet-up spot when I finally arrived at the cafeteria, out of breath with my hair in two haphazard braids. We were supposed to discuss the final details of the show before the big event the following weekend. Last night, my dreams were haunted by an empty auditorium or a few mean students who had only shown up to laugh and heckle.

Our goal was to earn Saffiya's fee for a semester's worth of dance classes and continue the fight through Student Council, hopefully with proof that the program a was good, meaningful addition to the campus culture. I hoped that students would show up for Janelle if not for the sake of watching African dance. She was the most popular Black girl on campus. Of course, behind her back, they called her a whore, but walking around campus, girls and guys, blacks, whites, and the sprinkling of other people of color around campus fawned over her and called out her name as she passed.

I was five minutes late, but surely Lucy couldn't have already eaten and left. It was unlike her to be late without a text or a call. I grabbed two bananas and decided to stop by Lucy's room before class. When I knocked on Lucy's door it creaked open at her touch.

"Lucy?" I called. A quiet moan like a dying animal emanated from the darkness within. I pushed the door, which creaked open at her touch.

"Lucy, are you alright?"

I knew my friend was not alright. The shades were drawn in Lucy's room, which was usually bright with different colored lamps, fairy lights, and Chinese lanterns. Now all was dark. The Ghanaian flag on the wall looked sinister in the shadows, the many gilded frames of family and friends appeared dim and lifeless. Clothing was strewn across the floor, books teetered in haphazard piles. Lucy was a mere lump under a heavy pink and white comforter. Her disheveled head peeked out from the bedding, eyeing me with sadness and suspicion. "Are you sick or something? You missed our breakfast date."

Cracking a nervous smile, I threw one of the bananas at her. Lucy made a small, pathetic moan as the fruit hit her midsection.

"Yes, I'm sick. Sorry, I should have texted you."

Her voice was hoarse. I took a step closer and saw her eyes were red with tears. "You've been crying?"

Lucy only breathed rattled breaths. Her teeth were clenched, holding back more tears.

Then I noticed a stain on the fitted sheet, where the comforter did not quite reach – red, and spreading towards the bed frame.

"Is that blood? Lucy, you're bleeding!" Her teeth still clenched, Lucy nodded.

I pulled back the comforter, which elicited a new sob from Lucy. Now I could see her thin, shaking body, her chaste and girlish white bra, the edges of which were stained yellow with sweat, and her blood-soaked underwear underneath which a blood-red sun reached its rays further and further out.

I could smell the blood, taste it thick in the air. Lucy had tried to ebb the flow with a sanitary pad, but it was not enough.

"Lucy, what happened? You need help!"

"They say it's normal. This is normal."

"Is it your period?"

Lucy slowly shook her head "no."

"I took the pill. I thought it would be easier than having a procedure."

Never before in life had I felt so small, so young, so utterly unprepared. Vague panicked thoughts ran through my mind. The hospital. Help. Friend dying on a twin xl bed in a darkened dorm room. The feeling of flesh-ripping instantly like the bike fender had torn her thigh outside of the Bashir's that night years ago. Alone, embarrassed, ashamed, pouring endless rivers of slick, sticky blood.

I felt my heart balance falter, but I would not allow my mind to escape. I needed to be there now with Lucy.

"When I got back from the clinic I tried to rest like the nurse said, but I couldn't sleep. I thought I would pass out from the cramps, but when I did, I had nightmares. I thought I would just stay here and wait for it to be over."

"What do you mean wait?" I asked, my stomach churning at the thought of her answer.

"Well, you're done waiting now. We have to get you cleaned up."

Lucy gave me a weak smile. "I have lots of chocolate, Celestine, in my drawer just there," her arm moved weakly towards the dresser. "Pass me some chocolate."

I did as I was told, taking a few squares of the dark chocolate Lindt bar for myself. We allowed the bittersweet candy to melt in our mouths, staining our teeth and coating our throats with sugary phlegm.

"This is better than anything they would give me at a doctor's office, or a hospital." she chuckled to herself, "Even if I could go."

There was truth in Lucy's words. Outside of the campus nurse, neither of us had affordable access to healthcare. It was a running joke among the international students, "Just don't get sick." My Caribbean grit made me believe this was possible. I could not stop staring at the pool of blood that threatened to engulf my friend. I broke off another piece of chocolate to soothe my racing mind.

"It will get better soon." I declared with no clue as to whether I was right or wrong. Lucy nodded. Even things as awful as this came to an end.

I ended up missing my morning class. I shuffled with Lucy to the girl's room to clean her off, flipped the mattress, and changed the soaked sheets.

Lucy nibbled at the banana and drank from her water bottle. Soon her spirits began to revive. She began to redirect all talk of her condition to the upcoming dance show.

"Feltman says he's not coming? Well, boohoo. What an ass. He tells you that like you should care. What an arrogant prick." she kissed her teeth.

"Do you think you'll be able to dance on Saturday?"

"Of course I will. Don't be silly. A Ghanaian woman is always ready to dance, don't talk nonsense."

"Be serious."

"I was born serious. My mother said I never cried and made a sour face when they jingled keys in front of my face. I was an unusual baby." I rolled my eyes.

"I'll be just fine, Celestine. By next week I'll think this was all a dream. At least I don't feel bloated."

"Thank God for that." I agreed. I did not ask how it happened or who was involved. I did not ask why Lucy decided the way she did. All of that had come to an end now. At the end of the day, after despair and deliberation, one has no choice but to move forward. No one knows that like Black girls.

23

Thursday evening, the night before the dance perfor-mance, Saffiya invited us to a dinner party at her house on the outskirts of Indianapolis. The dance girls had come to ac-cept me. Even Janelle sometimes smiled at my jokes, laughing in soft chuckles and finishing up with "you weird."

We piled in the back of Don's truck, our sweaty brown legs sticking to the hot leather seats.

"Don't you have air conditioning?" Lucy lamented.

"If it worked, don't you think it would be on?" he huffed.

Dark shadows were forming at the pits of his red polo shirt.

"Ya'll should just be grateful for the ride." he said, merging onto an endless interstate Highway.

"You were invited too." I pointed out. Don could only scowl at this. Saffiya wanted to meet the young man who had gone through so much trouble to secure the dance theater on a Saturday night. I was still not quite sure how he had done it, but I was afraid to ask too many questions.

When we arrived, Saffiya was busy in the kitchen. She called, "The door is open!" and we eagerly filed in making a beeline for the delicious smells coming from the kitchen. Saf-fiya's locs were wrapped in bright, intricate Kente cloth. She sashayed around the kitchen in a white apron, with smudges of orange-yellow yam and a dusting of cinnamon down the front. All around her, pots bubbled and sang. She had the radio tuned to the oldies station. "September" by

Earth, Wind, and Fire filled the kitchen. Don immediately made himself at home, kicking off his shoes by the door and sitting on one of the bar stools near the kitchen island. His eyes grew wide with the array of sweet-smelling pies and cakes lined up before him – pecan pie, sweet potato pie, peach cobbler, cornbread, and blackberry crumble.

"This looks delicious, Miss Saffiya." He said, never taking his eyes away from the delicious spread.

"Boy, you look like you haven't eaten anything proper in a long time." She said, looking him up and down.

"I know that's right," Janelle interjected. "Nothing but flavorless white people food on

campus. Now, I'm saying, how am I supposed to maintain this booty with bird food?" She gave her own backside a slap. Everyone laughed.

"And I even have vegan options for you, Pamela." Pamela grinned, happy to have someone acknowledge her alternative lifestyle which was usually the butt of a joke within the group. Even then, I could tell Janelle was holding back a quip about Pamela's carbon footprint t-shirt and environmentally sustainable sandals.

"Thank you, Miss Saffiya!" she squealed, pulling on one of her braided pigtails. This was my first real encounter with southern cuisine. The smells were intoxicating. I felt at home immediately, like I was ready to curl up in Saffiya's pillow and blanket-laden couch and stay forever.

She served us all tall glasses of lemon iced tea. I set about exploring the first floor of the house. Every nook of the space was decorated with framed photos, art prints, and abstract

sculptures. Many of the photos were of Saffiya herself many years ago, mid-pose or hanging on to the shoulder of a friend in a leotard. The fireplace mantle was dotted with small plaques and trophies from a full and passionate life.

I envied her. I could not see what my future would look like beyond the next 24 hours, and even that was proving to be unpredictable these days. I had no idea what I wanted for myself as a career. When I thought of success, I thought of wearing a suit and going to an office, possibly having a name-plate on a desk of my own. All of these images had come from television and movies and if moving to America had taught me anything, it was that movie scenes never lived up to expectations in reality. From the photographs and knick-knacks around her home, it appeared that Saffiya had truly lived a fulfilling life. I was still figuring out where to begin. Don found me in the foyer holding a framed photo of Saffiya and a Saxophone player in a porkpie hat.

"That woman has really lived," he said, observing the photo over my shoulder.

"Yeah," I sighed, "I hope I can do as much in my life."

"Oh yeah?" Don attempted to lean casually on the half-moon hall table, disturbing the crystal angel figurines so that I hastily moved to stabilize them. He stood up straight again. I grinned, noticing how awkward he was in any place that wasn't the football field.

"I can see you doing big things, Celestine. You could be a politician or something. Some kind of leader." Don suggested.

"Me?"

"Yes, you. What else are you in Student Council for? Can't be for fun."

"I honestly don't know why anymore. After this semester, I think I'm done."

"Done? Girl, whatchu mean? This is only the beginning. You're like our Michelle Obama."

I snorted at this.

"I'm no Michelle Obama. I'm not even a citizen." I lamented.

"That can change." Still, I shook my head.

"People would laugh at my accent."

Don sighed, "Someone will always be laughing somewhere. You can't let that stop you." he was relentless.

"And what about you, Don Bradford?"

I knew it was impolite to say it, but obviously, as a division two football player, he would not be going on to join the NFL.

"What about me?" he shrugged his massive shoulders. "My dad owns a car dealership down in New Orleans. I'm supposed to end up there, I think."

I shook my head slowly. "Wouldn't life be so simple if we all did what we were supposed to do?"

Dinner was everything that the smells had promised. Roasted chicken, collard greens, rice, and black beans, mashed potatoes, and green beans filled every plate around the oval dining room table. Looking around, it felt like the closest thing to a family dinner I had experienced since I was back home. Better, even. Just as Don picked up his fork and got ready to dig in, Saffiya grabbed his left hand and Lucy's right, bowing her head and signifying that we would pray first. My hand felt particularly small in Don's baseball mitt-sized embrace beneath the table, a peculiar sensation, half tickle, half electric shock, ran up my arm and whizzed around in my stomach. I concentrated on the soothing sound of Saffiya's voice.

"Lord, we gather here today to celebrate the hard work and sacrifice that these beautiful young people have put in all year long. Each and every one of them has been blessed with a special gift, and no matter what worldly forces try to obscure these talents, we know it is your will that they shine. And so it is! Lord, I pray you bless this food –."

Don muttered, "Lord, bless it!" under his breath, and I suppressed a giggle.

"And allow the recipes that nourished our ancestors to do the same for us tonight. Lord, I pray you bless us as we dance tomorrow night, bless the crowd that comes out to see us share our beautiful culture, bless the determined organizers who wouldn't take "no" for an answer because your "yes" is higher than any worldly authority. Thank you, God! Amen!" "Amen!" We all repeated.

There were a few minutes of relative quiet except for the clinking of cutlery, plates, and glasses as everyone tucked into the delicious meal. The first to start eating was also the first to start talking. Don addressed Naomi from across the table.

"I saw your last game, Naomi. Yo, you are a beast out there! I wasn't expecting that!"

Naomi pushed up her cat-eye glasses, smiling meekly. Naomi was on the lacrosse team. She was the only Black girl on the team, and it must have been difficult, but she never complained.

I was embarrassed to say I had never even heard of lacrosse

before coming to this campus and certainly had not been to any of her games.

"Yeah, I can get pretty intense during the game."

"I wish I could smack some of those snooty white girls with a stick," Janelle interjected, swilling her wine glass.

"It's not like that," Naomi said quickly.

"What did you say they told you the other day when you wore your hair out? You looked like a wild lion or some racist bullshit like that? Yeah, give me the stick." Ignoring Janelle, Saffiya leaned across the table with genuine interest.

"Do they really give you a hard time?"

"Yeah," she admitted, "But I'm there for the game, not to make friends. At least that's what my mom says."

"Thank goodness we are your friends!" Lucy chimed, raising her own glass of wine. Cheers of agreement sounded around the table and everyone clinked glasses. Somehow this felt more real than anything I had ever experienced with Gerty, Caitlyn, and Margo. I felt that with these girls, and maybe even Don too, I could survive here a little longer. After dinner, the drinks began to flow.

"Not too much! Don, you have to get these ladies back to campus safely! And ladies, I want to see you in tip-top shape for tomorrow night's performance!" Saffiya lectured.

The DJ was playing 90s hits on the hip-hop station, and as one would expect in a room full of dancers, bodies began to move. The girls sang along to TLC and rapped with Missy. I felt lost at times, not having grown up with the music in the same way as the rest of them. Sure, we sometimes caught American stations on our crackling radio, and Anika collected mixed tapes from her many cool friends, but I could not identify with hearing these songs at family gatherings or on the way to school every morning. After my second glass of wine, my head was spinning, an unfamiliar song was playing, and I made my way towards the bathroom. Don stopped me in the hallway, holding my elbow gently.

"Can I have this dance, Miss Celestine?"

I laughed nervously.

"I don't think so. I can't really dance."

"Sure you can. I've seen you at parties before."

I shook my head, "Let me write you a rain check." I said as sweetly as possible. One had to be as sweet as possible to avoid the off chance that the guy became angry. I had learned that lesson early on here from the rare occasion I was asked to dance.

"Alright then," he took it well. "I cash my rainchecks, though. Don't think I'll forget."

With that, he headed back to the living room. In the bathroom, I splashed my face and looked in my reflection. Every time I looked at her, I saw something different depending on my mood. Tonight, she was smooth, supple brown skin, long eyelashes, and an undecided mouth. I closed my lips tight, then I relaxed my features and let my mouth hang open, the way it seemed to go naturally. Anika had always accused me of being a "mouth breather". I thought my face might be passable tonight, even good looking at certain angles, I turned my head this way and that. Even daring to admire myself seemed like an act of rebellion. I could ignore the lingering truth of not enough and pretend to be beautiful.

I allowed myself to think that it had been a good night. Good food, good company. I allowed myself to think, for a fleeting moment of Don. It seemed that he might possibly like me, although the concept of any man truly being interested in me still seemed foreign and certainly flawed. And maybe, I could like him too, if I allowed myself to get past my self-loathing and put myself out there again. Again. I could not help but remember the last time I felt flutters of love and hope. I was still stamping out the burning embers beneath my bare heels. I decided not to think of him tonight. I gave my face one more splash and got ready to re-enter the party.

Before I could reach the living room, I heard the unmistakable sound of Janelle's flirty voice.

"So, you like Celestine or something?"

Don made a strange sound. Not quite a laugh, not quite a grunt with a question mark at the end.

"She's alright if you like that type. You know she likes white boys, right?"

I moved up the hall quietly. Peeking around the bend from the shadows, I could see the two pressed together on the love seat, Janelle's legs crossed and exposed in an exaggerated manner, her arm flung over his shoulders.

"I'm not worried about that," Don said in a low voice, his eyes staring, unfocused into the kitchen

"I'm just tryna warn you. I don't want you to get your heartbroken. Plus, she's kinda wack, you know? Boring if you ask me."

Don turned to her finally. Janelle smacked her lips so that her glitter gloss shone anew. "Good thing I didn't ask you, then."

Her sexy demeanor cracked in two. Just at that moment,

Pamela who had ventured near the two to collect her charging cell phone spotted me in the hallway. She yawned loudly.

"I'm getting tired," she announced suddenly, "Plus, I have an 8 am Environmental Science class to get to."

Janelle had gone from hurt to angry in a flash.

"It's sophomore year and your dumb ass is still taking 8 am classes?" she snapped at Pamela.

Pamela crossed her arms defiantly.

"Some of us are morning people." she spat.

On the ride home, everyone was drunk and tired except for Don, who as promised, stayed alert with his eyes on the road. At one point, when we were nearing campus, the car came to a sudden halt, jolting everyone out of their stupor. In the headlights, we watched a baby deer and her mother canter across the road with slow dignity. Nobody said anything, although we could hear each other breathing loudly.

"Just a doe and her youngin', ladies. Nothing to fear."

We all sat back, relieved, and Don drove on. Soon the rest of the girls fell asleep, but I was still shaken up. Something about the creature springing out into the road in the black of night made me feel queasy and vulnerable to the unexpected in life. I pulled my cardigan tight around my shoulders. The steamy day had turned into a chilly evening.

"You're really pulling this off, Celestine," Don said, his eyes on the road.

"Thank you for believing in me and helping."

"Yeah, what's life without believing? It's like that song 'Don't Stop Believing'" he sang.

I laughed, "I've never heard that song before."

"You've never heard 'Don't Stop Believing?'" You're joking, right? By Journey?"

"No, I'm not. I suppose you're right. But there's still plenty of time for things to go wrong."

"Don't talk like that. You're putting bad juju out in the universe."

"You care about juju?"

"All I know is you gotta be careful with words. From your lips to God's ears. It's gonna be a great event. That's final."

Don found 'Don't Stop Believing' on his iPod, making their back to campus feel like the start of an epic adventure.

24

At half-past five, I was speed walking down to Price Hall, toting three different bulky bags filled with supplies for any circumstance or mishap. Tape, cables, a first aid kit, the programs (all folded with anxious precision) a six-foot banner, and more. When I was halfway to my destination, my phone began to ring, which gave me such a start that I dropped the banner. Setting my other bags down on a nearby bench, I picked up the poster, blowing off some stray dirt, and answered the phone.

It was Saffiya. Apparently, there was a mix-up at the venue, and Price Hall was actually closed for renovations. Although she had not said so, I knew exactly who was behind this sudden change in plans. Sure enough, when I stormed onto the lawn of Price Hall, Jason and Alex were standing with their arms crossed, a group of 10-15 of their closes knucklehead friends standing behind them as Saffiya and the dance team pleaded with them. As I approached, both parties went quiet.

"What's going on here? Price Hall is suddenly closed for renovation?"

"It's not really so sudden. You may not have been aware. I understand that you didn't book this space through official means. You called in a favor?"

Jason spoke through his teeth, presumably to prevent himself from grinning too widely.

"Don did. And he told me that everything was finalized."

"Well, Don was wrong. You really have to learn how to follow the rules, Celestine. Policy and procedure exist for a reason. You would think you would understand that by now, seeing as you're on the student council."

I marched up to the heavy wooden doors of Price Hall and pulled at them with all of my strength. They were locked. Jason dangled a set of keys in the air.

"So, it's "closed" for renovation and the school just happened to send you, a student, to

lock it up?"

"I'm not just a student. I'm student council president."

I could not help but crack a smile; his smugness was hilarious. Jason's eyes narrowed, and his chest puffed up beneath his blue polo shirt.

I spotted Don's unmistakable beefy build approaching Price from a distance. He did not hesitate to walk up to Jason directly. The two were less than arm's length apart. I stepped back, sensing the instant rise in testosterone.

"What's the problem here?" Don asked gruffly.

"This place is closed for renovation. Calling in favors does not make a reservation, Don. When are you people going to learn how things are done?" Don ignored that quip. He tried to explain.

"I didn't just call in a favor, I spoke to the campus buildings manager. He assured me that –."

"Yeah, well, whatever he assured you wasn't on the books." Jason shook his head.

"What happened to you, Don? You used to be cool fresh-man year. You never cared about any of this shit. Ever since Jamaican Barbie showed up, she's got you all messed up. I mean, she's not my type, but she seems to have power over certain guys on campus …you're not the first." Jason smirked, his clever eyes dancing with cruel glee. His posse laughed and jeered. Don grabbed Jason by the collar of his polo shirt, pulling him so close that the two were eye to eye. Jason's limbs flailed wildly, his face red and mouth twisted into a sneering smile.

I stepped in between the two.

"Don, please. It's not worth it." I gently pulled him away from Jason and his friends. In a low tone, I said to him, "The show will go on one way or another. We don't need you get-ting in trouble. There's only one way a situation like that ends and that's with you in jail or worse."

Don's forehead was shiny with sweat, he looked like his mind was somewhere else completely. I tried to connect with him, touching him lightly on the shoulder which seemed to bring him back.

Red-faced and huffing with adrenaline, Jason stumbled back to his lame crew of so-called friends who had not even attempted to step in and defend him.

"Coward," he spat, retreating back to the steps of Price Hall, and placing his hands on his hips as if he alone could guard the venue. His friends, confused on what to do, scat-tered. Some even joined the growing crowd of people sitting cross-legged on jackets and grass, waiting for the show to be-gin.

As our audience began to approach the hall, Saffiya and

the dancers were already welcoming and redirecting them to the lawn. Saffiya sashayed gracefully into the middle of the circle. Before this point, I hadn't fully taken in the beauty of her flowing purple robes which fluttered with her every movement. Two men who I recognized as Saffiya's nephews, held drums between their knees and played beautiful rhythms that one could feel pulsating in the night air.

Around the dance team, students, faculty, and staff began to gather. From freshman to senior, from the physics department to the English department, the school began to gather around and more seemed to arrive in droves. I spotted several of my professors. Even Professor Hall surveyed the scene with an air of skepticism, standing back to see what would happen.

The show covered every aspect of Black music and dance. They started off with traditional African dance which melted into jazz, into soul, into rock n roll, and then Motown. I was just as awestruck as I was every time I saw the team perform. How had they learned to do so many different styles of dance? How could they make it look so easy, so natural? Swinging each other from left to right, and dancing slow and sensual to classic Bob Marley songs. By the end of the performance, they had come to the modern-day hip-hop and R&B hits that the crowd could sing along to. The music was so good that several pockets of the lawn had broken out in dance. By the time darkness began to descend upon the performance, it had the vibe of a festival rather than a show.

After the show, Saffiya projected her voice so that all gathered could hear, and the people on the fringes of the crowd gathered in closer to hear.

"I want to thank you all for coming out tonight. These talented young ladies you see all around me have been working hard all year." The crowd burst into applause at this. The girls were beaming.

"Yet they would have never had the opportunity to showcase their talents if it weren't for Celestine Samuels. Celestine? Come up here!"

The crowd parted ways for me to pass. When I reached the circle, I slipped between Pam and Lucy, who both gave me encouraging pats on her shoulders. I stood next to Saffiya. For the first time, I could see the true scope of the crowd. A good chunk of the campus was here and they were all looking on with excitement, joy, and admiration. I thought she might faint.

"Is there anything you want to say, Celestine?" Saffiya asked.

"I just want to say... thank you and I... wow this is actually happening." I spotted Don's face in the crowd. "And I guess... don't stop believing." The crowd roared with appreciation and merriment.

I took the opportunity to bring around a clipboard and ask people to sign a petition for Saffiya to stay. I approached one older white man in a plaid sports jacket with wisps of gray hair floating above his balding head and smiled, ready to hand him the clipboard to sign the petition. Graciously, he held out a hand to signal his refusal. Feeling somewhat awkward, I began to turn away.

"You're Celestine Samuels, aren't you?" he called in a clear, but gentle voice. I turned around and nodded, "Yes, that's me."

"Your reputation precedes you, young lady. My name is

John Brockman, I'm the chairman of the school's Board of Trustees."

I could not think of what to say besides, "Wow. I'm honored to meet you."

He smiled and nodded modestly as if acknowledging that it was indeed an honor.

"That proposal you sent in caused quite a fuss among the board. I don't think we've had a meeting that interesting for ten years or more!" he laughed and so I laughed too.

"I didn't mean to cause any trouble. I just felt it needed to be said." John furrowed his thick, gray eyebrows.

"Never be afraid to cause trouble, Celestine. This country was built by trouble makers." he winked.

"Anyway, I wanted to see what all of the passion and protest was about. I thought it would be a good idea for a few board members and myself to come to the performance and see the dancers as well as the dance teacher everyone seems to love so much. I understand what you all see in her. Saffiya is a lovely woman, one of a kind, truly. If I weren't such an old geezer, I'd ask her out to dinner tonight. Heck, I might still..."

The old man reddened and straightened his bow tie.

"But back to the subject at hand. I think you made some great points, Celestine. We need to do more for the marginalized groups on campus. Problem is, a bunch of rich old white dudes are not exactly in touch with what the students need. That's why we need leaders like you to speak up in order to make changes. I think the first change will be hiring Saffiya as an Associate Professor so that she can teach dance here. What do you think?"

I almost couldn't believe I was hearing him correctly. My head fervently nodded "yes" before my mouth could catch up.

"That would be amazing! If it's alright with her, of course!"

"Yes, I'll go ahead and make the offer. She seems like a lady who likes to make up her own mind."

While Mr. Brockman was lost in thought, psychoanalyzing the new object of his affection, I was so filled with glee that I thought I might burst. Unsure of what that might look like, I thanked Mr. Brockman again and excused myself. The clipboard in my hands was now useless and I held back the urge to sing. Never before had I been embraced by the campus the way that they embraced me that night. Near the back doorway of Price Hall, I overhead two familiar voices.

"What should I have done? That's just the way she is." Margo protested, her voice hoarse

in between pulls of a Camel cigarette.

"You could have, I don't know, defended me." said Patty. She sounded as if she had been crying.

"How the hell was I supposed to defend you when I couldn't even defend myself? Do you think this is the first time this has happened?"

"That she's found you with another girl?"

"No, that she's beaten me. See this... this is the difference between you and me. What should I have done? Taken her to family therapy? Called CPS? Told a "good" police officer so they can deport my family?" I heard the familiar sound of Margo sobbing, a sound I often woke up to in the middle of the night.

I backed away from the scene only to bump directly into Gerty. Her face was pale and makeupless. She had had never looked more sober. We searched each other's faces for a moment, and then, me feeling nothing, I turned to walk away.

"Wait, Celestine."

I waited.

"I feel like this has all spun out of control."

"I'm not sure I know what you mean."

"Me, Jason, you, this show."

Was I supposed to figure it out? Piece together my own apology from Gerty's tone and sad facial expressions? Gerty called upon my apologetic nature, my innate need to understand and heal. But I was beginning to understand that this was a gift, a virtue that not everyone deserved and was mine to give.

"I have to go now," I said in a low voice. Gerty's eyes were wide and pleading.

That night, I tagged along with the dance team to Don's apartment where a birthday party for his roommate was already in full swing. I almost felt bad for the guy, because the dance girls were by far the most popular people in the room. Fellow students clamored to get a chance to congratulate them and praise their performance. Janelle was completely in her element, nodding along to compliments with practiced grace and charm. The more introverted girls like Pam and Naomi seemed exhausted by the attention, but happy nevertheless. I received my own fair shares of "good job" and "amazing work" from people, many of whom I'm sure had thought me a menace only a few days ago. The results were what had changed minds. I understood more and more that only very few encourage the underdog along the way, but when you produce results, suddenly people see you.

After we all sang happy birthday to Sam, a boy on the football team I had only seen in passing, the dance girls ushered me outside, far enough away from the party that our voices could be heard over the music.

"We have something for you, Celestine!"

"For me? I can't imagine what."

Lucy made a "tut tut" sound. "Always so skeptical. Just wait."

Janelle pulled out a folded paper from her purse and handed it to me. A roundtrip ticket to Georgetown Guyana and back.

"We know you haven't been able to afford to go home since you got here and since Saffiya was offered – and has accepted by the way – a faculty position at the school, we figured you could use the proceeds from the concert. She doesn't need it anymore!"

Mouth opened, I looked around at the group in disbelief. I almost wanted to give it back. Lucy seemed to read my mind.

"No ifs or buts. You deserve it. Go and see your family. This place will drive you mad if you stay for too long."

They all enclosed me in a hug. I felt my eyelashes grow heavy and then my cheeks become wet. I had no words.

"Come on! Don't be crying and shit." Janelle offered in what I realized was her comforting tone. "You're gonna be all red-eyed and we're about to go back in there. I know somebody in there's tryna spend a little more time with you if you know what I mean."

On the way back to the party, I fell back from the crowd and looked up at the sky. Long before I recognized the outlines of stately buildings or the rise and fall of the campus landscape, I was intimately familiar with the stars in the same night sky. Many nights back home, I sat in a yellow, painted rocking chair near my bedroom window and gaze out at the infinite night sky. My grandfather had taught me the constellations, but I could never really get them straight and part of me wanted to believe that there was a place my eyes could perceive without rules and order, a grand mystery waiting for me to solve it. As long as there was something to wonder about, life was still worth living. That night I concluded that somehow some way, there had to be a God.

25

As the plane touched down at Cheddi Jagan International Airport, the feeling of dread had been growing in my throat for the entire plane ride, making me choke on the dry biscuits the flight attendant had given out. She was afraid that she had changed too much. I listened to the voices of the two women seated behind her, their thick accents flowing with excitement over a wedding they were to attend, and hoped that my own accent would return once I stepped foot on Guyanese soil and that the learned, nasally white girl talk she had adapted would disappear with the Indiana landscape. I was different now, but at the same time, she was afraid of people telling me so. In my experience, when someone came back home from the United States or England or Canada, folks tended to look at them askance, as if asking what had really brought them back from the land of opportunity, as if asking what there was to really miss in this country. At that point, it was advisable to pull out some gifts, little bits of America to make people understand that they had not been forgotten even while their friend or relative had been caught in the whirlwind of American abundance. It struck me how backward this viewpoint was. Most of the Caribbean immigrants she had known in America were working day and night and still not living glamorous lives. Sure, for the most part, they could rely on electricity, running water, and a dizzying amount of colorful options at the local grocery store, but immigrant life was far from a life of leisure. I had watched Aunt Sylvia's neighbors fill blue barrels with food and supplies to send back when it was obviously difficult enough for them to stock their own cupboards, all because they knew at some level that even their meager earnings would be a blessing to families back home. Maybe that was where my own shame came from.

All of the problems I had encountered at school, boy trouble, discrimination, loneliness, and dejection, seemed like nothing when compared to the life or death issues in Guyana which I had once assumed were par for the course. I understood why people moved away and did not come back. Once one emerged from the choppy water and was able to stop flailing and breathe a clear breath, why on earth would you choose anything else? Even I had opted to only stay for two weeks. I had a job as a camp counselor waiting for me back in Brooklyn once July started. The heat of the land embraced me as soon as I stepped off of the plane. Joey had come to pick me up. He was driving Uncle Marvin's old car as a taxi now.

"Celestine! It's so good to see you, sis!" he picked up my suitcase and placed it in the trunk, slamming the hatch closed and giving the back of the car a slap.

"It's good to see you too. I never thought I would say it, but I missed you."

"Are you kidding me? I knew you would miss me. I'm the life of the party."

Joey still had the same lazy laugh, but he had grown in the last two years, his body had filled out so that he no longer had boyish willowy limbs. He had even grown a patchy beard which I could not quite take seriously, but I knew better than to joke about it. When a man grows a beard, it's serious business.

"So, you're a taxi driver now?"

"I am many things, sister. I'm a hustler baby!" he sang.

My laugh quickly turned to a shriek when a man with his face covered in a black bandana came running up beside the car, slamming his fist on the top of the old Toyota yelling "Give me the money! Give me the money!" into the passenger side window.

Joey stopped the car.

"Chill out, Tony. This is my sister! My sister!" Tony's eyes widened with this realization.

"My bad partna." he said to Joey, "How are you miss Celestine?"

It took me a moment to realize that I knew Tony and that he had been over to the house several times in the past. He and Joey had gone to school together. "I was fine before all of this commotion."

"Jus a simple mix-up, Cele. How was school in America? You come back for good now? I mus say, you looking good gyal."

Joey cleared his throat. "Now is not a good time. Listen, we gon link up later, okay?"

Tony nodded and jogged away towards some bushes. Joey started driving again. They turned ton to the main road, the car rocking up and down on potholes, moving no faster than donkey carts and motorcycles on either side.

"Wow, you were not kidding about being a hustler!" Joey smiled nervously.

"Yeah, we have a few little tricks we play. First, it started off just selling what the passengers drop di the car. Then Tony say he can help double my money if I can give he a cut and… it works."

At home, the sweet aroma of Guyana's best soup wafted out from inside the house. Pulling up to the faded coral house, a sense of unexpected longing filled my chest and panged so acutely, it almost hurt. I leaped out of the car as soon as the sputtering engine stopped. Our little dog, Rufus, jumped and barked at the rusted gate which I pushed open with the usual downward jig. The tiny flea-bitten dog hopped in circles around my feet barking incessantly until Joey groaned, "Be quiet, yuh ugly dog!"

With all of the commotion, I saw mom's face in the screen door, already beaming as she swung the door open to welcome me. She called back into the house, "She's here" and to my surprise, my sister bounded to the front of the house. Aunt Zoe came forward with her usual long, graceful steps, a smile spreading slowly across her lips. Mom held me close, kissing the side of my head as she teetered from side to side.

"Ah, my girl!" she sighed into my ear, "I missed you yuh know!"

After a few more hard kisses, she released me to Anika, who hugged me tightly for only a few short seconds and then let go as if embarrassed, beaming at me appreciatively. Then, of course, Aunt Zoe embraced me and whispered, "Welcome home" the words I didn't know I needed to hear.

Standing back all three of them looked so different, so changed. Mom had cut her hair short and close to her head. A small afro, thinning at the edges gave her a smart, clean look, emphasizing her pointy cheekbones and deep-set eyes. She stood a little bit straighter than I remembered, a figure a little bit fuller. She looked well.

Anika was also changed. Her long extensions were nowhere to be found. Instead, her partially relaxed natural hair was gathered into two French braids joined at the ends. She wore a faded cricket t-shirt and cotton shorts. For the first time, my older sister looked younger than me and seemed comfortable with it. Aunt Zoe, too, had gone through a transformation, although her change in appearance made me wary. She was skinnier, her skin grayer, she smiled as if she had nearly forgotten how.

Much of her hair had broken at the ends and the remains were gathered into a straw-like ponytail. In a faded house-dress, she resembled a spirit, a soul already partially departed, but lingering around the periphery of life.

"I made soup!" Mom announced, clapping her hands together to break the awkwardness of my lingering stare. We all happily followed her to the kitchen table.

"Tony almost rob us yuh know!" Joey was slurping and talking at once. "What a jokester."

"It is not a joke." Mom sparred with him, using her usual, fake-threatening tone, "You boys need to sharpen up. Look at Kelvin. That boy is doing it right, I tell you." I raised my eyebrow with interest.

"Uhhuh Celestine, your boyfriend is hot stuff now." Anika laughed into her soup.

"Don't laugh!" Mom admonished, "He is in the police academy now. Young lad will be a policeman soon!"

I made an impressed sound, but I was not surprised. Marvin had always been the type to take himself seriously. Policeman seemed like a fitting profession.

"Cele has a new boyfriend now. A white boy." Anika smiled wickedly.

"Eh eh!" Mom exclaimed in fake surprise. Surely Anika had not been sitting on this hot topic for so long. The whole table was in giggles.

"Sister, I warned you to stay away from the white man. I tell you something ain't right with them. You can't trust em!" Joey said, crossing his arms. I wondered if he knew how right he was.

"We're not together anymore. That was over a long time ago." I told the table, ears turning hot.

"I bet she has a new boyfriend now!" Once she got started, she was unstoppable. I shook my head, *no*, "I'm a single lady."

"Now that's what I like to hear! Focused on her studies! Right, Zoe?" Mom turned to her sister, who had been mostly silent.

"Right." She offered another fragile smile.

After dinner, I caught up with Anika, who seemed softer now, more open. We sat in the bed we used to share. I understood that she now shared the bed with Aunt Zoe, who would share with mom now that I was back for a visit.

Laying by my sister's side and letting a cool breeze blow in from the window, I felt I never wanted to be anywhere else in the world ever again. We listened to the rhythm of the insects and birds for a short while before she began.

"Well, spill it. I want to know everything."

"It's hard to know where to start." Indeed, looking back,

the past two years had the ephemeral and slightly implausible nature of a dream to it.

"America is... so many things at once. Like sensory overload."

"You have a lot of new friends." She offered.

I nodded.

"Some better than others. It's strange, It's like it doesn't matter how many people you know. At the end of the day, you're still alone. It's strange." I was eager to change the subject.

"What's going on with you and... that guy."

"It's over." She sounded crestfallen. "He start tellin me about wife and ting and how she find out he talking to girls on the internet. Girls, not just me, girls. He was a liar. I don't think he was ever going to fly me over to America." Her voice lowered, embarrassed.

"Maybe it's for the best. Bad things happen in America too, yuh know."

Anika nodded silently.

"I been going back to school." She said quickly, like a confession.

"That's great, sis."

"Yeah, I started working a few shifts cleaning at the hospital. I think I want to be a nurse. I have a friend, Chandra, who is a nurse and she said I can be one too if I finish school and get a little training. I like to be with the babies in the nursery. I sing to them."

"I bet they love it."

"They make a better audience than the sleazy guys at the clubs in Georgetown. That is for sure!" We laughed.

I decided not to tell Anika, mom or Aunt Zoe about my plans the next day. I wouldn't have included Joey if I didn't need a ride so badly. After breakfast, I showed him the address, ripped from the envelope that had made it all the way to Indiana.

"Why yuh need to go there?" Joey asked, scrunching up his face. "This place is in the bush. You know somebody there?"

I placed my finger on my lips, imploring him with my eyes to lower his voice.

"I'll tell you on the way." I pleaded. If I had been home for a few more weeks, the plea might not have worked, but he was still willing to indulge me.

In the car, we drove down busy city streets into the sparsely populated county. The roads turned to dirt and houses grew far in between. Lush forest and vegetation threatened to take over whatever land humans had staked out.

"So, what's all of this about?" Joey demanded.

"Our father."

He was silent for a moment, his lips tight together. Then he said, "Our father is dead, Celestine."

"You don't actually believe that, do you? That's just what mom told us."

"And for good reason." Joey's voice grew unexpectedly angry. He cleared his throat as if he hadn't expected the change in tone either.

"So you knew? You knew it was all a lie?" Joey kept his eyes on the bumpy country road.

"Do you know what it is like to grow up in the shadow of that kind of man? The way people around the neighborhood talked about him… he was a disgrace. I had to prove myself to be a man without even knowing what a man is yet. No one to teach me." I didn't say anything.

"It's different for you. You are a girl. You are the baby. Sometimes, people don't lie. Sometimes, people protect. There is a difference. One is love."

We pulled up to a farmhouse. A teenage girl sat on the front steps, washing clothes in a bucket with foul clucking and squawking loudly in the yard before her. Joey would not let me go alone.

The girl stared wide-eyed at me as if I were an alien. My style of dress was chic even for Georgetown and outlandish in the country. Joey worried someone would rob me, figuring I was an American. He would know.

"Hello, good afternoon." I started.

"Hello," the girl said in little more than a whisper. She held a shirt mid scrub against the washboard.

"I'm looking for Alton. I heard he was staying here."

The girl raised her eyebrows, alarmed.

"No, no! Not he! Not here! He gone. Whatever trouble have nothing to do with we." She began sputtering.

"I am his daughter."

Her eyes widened even further.

"Ahah! His American daughta!"

A part of me felt like explaining that I was not American, but I knew what she meant.

Trying to explain otherwise would have been pointless. I had been touched by the place.

"Where is he now?" I asked.

Her wistful expression left quickly. The girl's eyes dropped into the washing bucket.

"He is dead, miss."

"Dead?"

"He drink di poison an die. He wanted to go. A man like he... it was a life full ah shame. No peace in life and no peace in death."

My mind went blank. I could not think of what to do or say next except take one breath and then the next.

"They come an take away the body. Mussa burn he up, no point in a burial."

Finally, I managed, "Did he leave anything?"

"Nothing, miss, he had nothing. Not even his words." She looked off into the distance.

"But... oh! I lie!" she stood up and ran into the house, gesturing for me to wait. She came back with a photograph held in front of her. I took it.

The house was young and freshly painted coral pink. Mom and Dad stood in the back row, his right arm around her shoulders. In the other hand, he held a baby girl in a frilly, blue dress with one chubby arm reaching out towards the camera. Anika was posing, hands on her hips like a movie star, in front of her parents. Joey had his arms crossed, refusing to smile. This was us, long, long ago.

I thanked the girl. In the car on the way back, I wept loudly. Even Joey shed a few silent tears. At home, I placed the photograph on the kitchen table as I sat with my head in my hands. I couldn't stop crying. The photo attracted every family member to the table. Gradually, they all sat, turning the photo in their hands as if assessing its weight, its reality, its authenticity. Anika looked upset, but turned to Joey, still confused.

"He is dead."

It was a strange announcement.

An announcement of what had before been a false truth, but was now a real truth, a rude disruption of the fantasy.

Mom put her arm around me.

"I never meant to hurt you..." she began. I nodded. Crying into her shoulder, I told my mother that I loved her.

That night, I cried myself to sleep. Laying in bed. I listened to the sounds of infinite chirps and rustles outside and tried to imagine myself safe and submerged in the nightwater surrounded only by the things that comforted my imagination. The nightwater had become crowded with new things, new faces. Inexplicably, Richard was there, his eyes pleading silently for forgiveness, a complete invasion of the space I could not ignore. Dance extravaganza posters floated all around, reminders of how far into the margin my body had been pushed and the hard work necessary to reassert my humanity, embarrassingly hard work. There are books, textbooks barely skimmed that feel more like lead weights on my chest, and loneliness tied in a neat bow around my neck pulled tighter and tighter. I cannot conjure the good things to comfort me. I realize with a startling turn in my stomach that I cannot remember my grandfather's face anymore. For the first time, the nightwater feels like it might suck me under, folding my body limb by limb with the full strength of the ocean currents.

I open my eyes, gasping. The room is dark. Anika sleeps gently next to me. I creep out of the bedroom and make my way to the living room, hoping to catch my breath, touch a few family keepsakes, and remember myself. Only I am not alone. Aunt Zoe is sitting in the rocking chair her face bathed in the glow of a smartphone.

"Goodnight Aunty," I say quietly.

Startled, she jumps a little before smiling at me.

"Goodnight Celestine"

I moved to her side. Before I left, I felt like more her daughter than my own mother, but she has been distant since my return. I tried not to take it personally as she did not seem to be connecting with anyone anymore.

"What are you up to?" I asked casually.

She looked me full in the face, deciding how much to reveal. It's a far cry from the old days when we gossiped like school girls.

"I'm talking to a friend, an old professor actually, in England."

"Oh wow."

"Yes," her shoulders relaxed, "Your Mr. Bashir put me on to the idea. Now Tommy, err Professor Miller - is asking if I'd like to come and assist him with some research."

"That's amazing, Aunty. Do you think you'll go?" she looked away into the darkness of the room.

"I can't go on anymore... not here... anymore," she said quietly.

I understood.

"You could go on there. Back in England, couldn't you?" The old spark seemed to return to her if only a flicker.

"Yes, I think I could go on there."

The next day would have been Uncle Marvin's 50th birthday. I felt awful that I had to be reminded. My mind was already consumed with death. I was numb to the prospect of grieving one more life. I had never been particularly fond of Uncle Marvin in life. In death, he had come to symbolize so much more, a turning point in all of our lives. I felt reverence for him if not affection. He was a man of principles, worthy of respect. This was why I cringed to see his grave overgrown with weeds and plant life. Mom wiped sweat from her face and chest as two boys hacked away at the tall grass with rusty cutlasses. The headstone was simple so as not to attract the attention of grave robbers.

Marvin Robert Hunter

July 7th 1958 – October 23rd, 2018

Husband, Change Maker

Aunt Zoe rested some flowers on the grave, dry-eyed and unsentimental. She had cried enough.

I closed my eyes and said goodbye to him as I had never truly had the chance. I thanked him. I was not sure why I thanked him until I found myself lost in thought on the drive home. I remembered Don Bradford and the earnestness in his voice when he told me *"I can see you doing big things, Celestine. You could be a politician or something. Some kind of leader."* I opened my eyes and scanned the familiar landscape. I thought to myself, "How ridiculous!", but could not prevent my lips from curling into a mischievous grin.

Thank you for reading!

Curious to know more about the world of *Departure Story*?

Visit us online for word definitions, related blogs, and a playlist you'll love!

Follow us on Instagram, Facebook & Twitter @Spoken-blackgirl

And of course, every review on Amazon and Goodreads helps!

Thanks for joining us on the journey!

Spokenblackgirl.com